"Before we go a
you should know
conditions."

Conditions?

"Is that so?" Taking a step toward Imma, Vicenzu held her gaze.

She nodded. "The marriage will last a year. That's long enough for it to look real, and for the media to lose interest. And if we manage our diaries, then we shouldn't have to intrude into one another's lives beyond what's necessary."

He stared at her in silence. All his life, women had fawned over him, flattered and chased him. But now Imma was basically treating him like a footstool.

"I have a condition, too," he said silkily.

Watching the slow color rise to her cheeks, he felt a flicker of satisfaction.

Louise Fuller was a tomboy who hated pink and always wanted to be the prince—not the princess! Now she enjoys creating heroines who aren't pretty pushovers but are strong, believable women. Before writing for Harlequin she studied literature and philosophy at university, and then worked as a reporter on her local newspaper. She lives in Tunbridge Wells with her impossibly handsome husband, Patrick, and their six children.

Books by Louise Fuller

Harlequin Presents

Vows Made in Secret
A Deal Sealed by Passion
Claiming His Wedding Night
Blackmailed Down the Aisle
Surrender to the Ruthless Billionaire
Revenge at the Altar
Craving His Forbidden Innocent

Secret Heirs of Billionaires

Kidnapped for the Tycoon's Baby
Demanding His Secret Son
Proof of Their One-Night Passion

Passion in Paradise

Consequences of a Hot Havana Night

Visit the Author Profile page
at Harlequin.com for more titles.

Louise Fuller

THE TERMS OF THE SICILIAN'S MARRIAGE

Recycling programs
for this product may
not exist in your area.

ISBN-13: 978-1-335-14879-7

The Terms of the Sicilian's Marriage

Copyright © 2020 by Louise Fuller

All rights reserved. No part of this book may be used or reproduced in
any manner whatsoever without written permission except in the case of
brief quotations embodied in critical articles and reviews.

This is a work of fiction. Names, characters, places and incidents
are either the product of the author's imagination or are used fictitiously.
Any resemblance to actual persons, living or dead, businesses,
companies, events or locales is entirely coincidental.

This edition published by arrangement with Harlequin Books S.A.

For questions and comments about the quality of this book,
please contact us at CustomerService@Harlequin.com.

Harlequin Enterprises ULC
22 Adelaide St. West, 40th Floor
Toronto, Ontario M5H 4E3, Canada
www.Harlequin.com

Printed in U.S.A.

THE TERMS OF THE SICILIAN'S MARRIAGE

For my wonderful husband, Patrick.
Still impossibly handsome, and still pressing
all the right buttons...

PROLOGUE

THE BAR WAS starting to empty.

Across the room, the blonde sitting at the counter with her friend looked over and gave Vicenzu Trapani a slow, lingering smile. A smile that promised a night, or quite possibly more, of unparalleled, uncomplicated pleasure.

Under normal circumstances he would have smiled back and waited for her to join him. But nothing was normal any more, and he wasn't sure he was ever going to smile again.

Picking up his glass, he stared down into the dark gold liquid. He didn't normally drink bourbon, particularly when he was back in Sicily, but it had been Ciro who had caught the bartender's attention. Ciro who had snapped out the order before Vicenzu's own numbed brain had even fully registered where they were. Ciro who had commandeered the table in the corner and pushed him into a seat.

They had left the meeting and come straight to the bar. Vito Neglia was their lawyer, and an old family friend, but today he had also been their last hope.

A hope that had been swiftly and brutally extinguished when Vito had confirmed what they already knew.

There was no loophole. Cesare Buscetta had acted within the law.

He was the new and legitimate owner of both the Trapani Olive Oil Company and the beautiful, beloved family estate where Vicenzu and Ciro had spent an idyllic childhood.

Vicenzu's fingers tightened around his glass. The family estate he still called home.

Home.

The word stuck in his throat and, picturing his mother's expression as he'd handed the keys over to the agent, he felt his stomach lurch.

It had broken his heart, having to do that to her, and the memory of her bewildered, tear-stained face would be impossible to forget. The reason for it impossible to forgive.

'We must fix this.'

Ciro's voice broke into his thoughts and, looking up, he met his brother's gaze—and instantly wished he hadn't.

Ciro's face was taut with determination, his green eyes narrow with a certainty he envied…eyes that so resembled their father's that he had to look away.

His stomach tightened. Ciro was his younger brother, but he was his father's son. Whip-smart, focused, disciplined, he could have taken over the business and run it with his eyes shut—hell, he could have turned it into a household name overnight. And, had their father been cut from different cloth, that was exactly what would have happened.

But Alessandro Trapani had not been a cut-throat man. To him, family had mattered more than global domination.

Or had it?

Vicenzu felt his stomach lurch again and, pushing away the many possible but all equally unpalatable answers to that question, he lifted his glass to his lips and drained it swiftly.

Meeting his brother's gaze, he nodded.

'We have to get it back. All of it.'

Ciro's voice was quiet, but implacable, and Vicenzu nodded again. His brother was right, of course. Cesare Buscetta was not just a thief, he was a bully and a thug. But it was too soon...feelings were still too raw.

He'd tried to explain that to his brother—had reminded him that revenge was a dish best served cold. Only Ciro couldn't wait—*wouldn't* wait. His need for vengeance was white-hot, burning him from the inside out. He wanted revenge *now* and he needed his brother to play his part.

'Vicenzu?'

For a moment he closed his eyes. If only he could turn back time. Give his father back the money he'd borrowed. Be the son his father had needed—wanted.

But regrets were not going to right the wrongs that had been done to his family and, opening his eyes, he leaned back in his chair and cleared his throat. 'Yes, I know what I have to do and I'll do it. I'll take the business back.'

His chest tightened. It sounded so simple—and maybe it would be. After all, all he had to do was get a woman to fall in love with him.

Only this wasn't *any* woman. It was Immacolata Buscetta—the daughter of the man who had hounded his father to death and robbed his beautiful, always-laughing mother of her husband and her home.

There was not much to go on. Cesare was a protective father, and by all accounts his eldest daughter was a chip off the old block—as ice-cold as she was beautiful. Who better than her to pay for the sins of her father?

He felt a sudden rush of fury. He would make her melt. Seduce her, then strip her naked—literally and metaphorically—and make her his wife. He would take back what belonged to his family and then, finally, when she was his—inside and out—she would discover why he had really married her.

A fresh round of drinks arrived and he picked up his glass.

Ciro's eyes met his. 'To vengeance.'

'To vengeance,' Vicenzu repeated.

And for the first time since his father's death he felt alive.

CHAPTER ONE

'Oh, my, doesn't she look beautiful?'

Without changing the direction of her gaze, Immacolata Buscetta nodded, her insides tightening with a mixture of love and sadness.

'Yes, she does,' she said softly, addressing her response to the Sicilian matron who was standing beside her, clutching her handbag against her body with quivering fingers.

Actually, privately she thought 'beautiful' was too mundane a word to describe her younger sister. Her stunning, full-skirted traditional white wedding dress was beautiful, yes, but Claudia herself looked beatific.

Not a word Imma had ever used before, and she would probably never use it again, but it was the only one that remotely came close to capturing the blissful expression on her sister's face.

Imma's heart gave a small twitch and she glanced over to where Claudia's new husband was greeting some of the one hundred carefully selected guests who had been invited to celebrate the marriage of Claudia Buscetta to Ciro Trapani on this near-perfect early summer's day in Sicily. There would be another hundred guests arriving for the evening reception later.

Of course Claudia was in a state of bliss. She had just married the man who had stormed their father's citadel and declared his love for her like some knight in a courtly romance.

But it wasn't Ciro's impassioned pursuit of her sister that was causing Imma's insides to tighten and her heart to beat erratically. It was the man standing next to the newlyweds.

Ciro's brother, Vicenzu, was the owner of the legendary La Dolce Vita hotel in Portofino. Like pilgrims visiting a shrine, members of royalty, novelists looking for inspiration, divas and bad boys from the world of music and film—all eventually made their way to his hotel.

Her throat tightened. And Vicenzu was the baddest of them all.

His reputation as a playboy and pleasure seeker stretched far beyond the Italian Riviera and it was easy to see why.

Reluctantly, her gaze darted towards him again, drawn like a moth to the flame of his absurdly beautiful features.

He was standing slightly to one side, taking advantage of an overhanging canopy of flower-strewn greenery, which made him both screened from view and yet still the most conspicuous person there.

With dark hair, a teasing mouth and a profile that would grace any currency, he stood out among the stocky Sicilian and Italian businessmen and their wives—and not just because he was a head taller than most of them.

Glancing up through her eyelashes, she felt a cool shiver tiptoe down her spine. In their formal suits and dresses, quite a few of the guests were perspiring beneath the heat of the sun, but he looked effortlessly cool, the impeccably fitted white shirt hugging his lean, supple body and perfectly setting off his dancing dark eyes.

At that moment he turned, and those same dancing eyes met hers, and before she had a chance to blink, much less move, he was sauntering towards her, a lazy smile pulling at the corners of his mouth.

'Immacolata...' He made a disapproving face. 'You don't play fair, do you, Ms Buscetta.'

'Play fair?' She stared up at him, her pulse beating with fear and fascination, trying to look calm and unaffected. How could he talk about being fair, looking like that? 'I don't understand.'

Up close, his beauty was so startling it felt like a slap to her face. His eyes, that beautiful, curving mouth, the clean-cut lines of his features... All made her mind go completely blank and made her feel bare, *exposed*, in a way that no other man ever had.

'Playing hide-and-seek without telling me...' He shook his head. 'That was sneaky.'

'I wasn't hiding,' she lied, desperately wanting to turn and walk away and yet held captive by the soft, baiting note in his voice. 'I was looking after my guests.'

'Not all of them,' he countered. 'I was feeling very neglected. Quite light-headed, actually. In fact, I think we might need to go somewhere quiet so you can put me in the recovery position.'

She felt her cheeks go red and, hating this instant and—worse—visible response to the easy pull of his words, she lifted her chin and glanced pointedly past his shoulder. 'There are cold drinks on the terrace, and plenty of seating.'

He grinned. 'Don't you want to know why I'm feeling so light-headed?'

'No, thank you. I'm perfectly fine as I am.'

'I couldn't agree more,' he said slowly.

As he spoke his eyes meandered over her body in a way that made her feel breathless and on edge. Fighting to keep control she glanced down at the lapel of his jacket. 'Vicenzu, I—'

His eyes glittered. 'It's okay. I get it. You thought I was just a pretty face, but now we've got to know each other a bit better you're starting to like me. It happens all the time. But don't worry—I'm not going to tell anyone.'

Her face flamed. 'Actually, I was just going to tell you that you've lost your boutonnière,' she said stiffly. 'Now, if you'll excuse me, I need to check on—on something. In the kitchen.'

Before he could say anything she turned and began walking blindly away from his mocking gaze, her panicky response to him echoing in her ears.

Panicky and prim and gauche.

Gritting her teeth, she smiled mechanically as people greeted her. What was the matter with her? She was an educated woman, had been top of her class at business school, and she was the daughter of one of the most powerful men in Sicily, soon to be CEO of her father's latest acquisition. So why had she fled like a rabbit from a fox?

But it hurt to look at him—and hurt even more to look away, even though that was what she'd been doing her very best to accomplish ever since he'd arrived at the church.

Only as they were maid of honour and best man,

there had been no avoiding his laughing dark eyes during the service.

It had been equally impossible not to be swept along by the beauty and romanticism of the ceremony, and as a shaft of sunlight had gilded his extremely photogenic features she had briefly allowed herself to fantasise that it was her wedding, and Vicenzu was her husband...

Her pulse twitched. It was nearly five years since she'd been remotely attracted to anyone, and her response to him was as shocking as it was confusing.

Three times she'd lost her place in the order of service, distracted by his gaze—a gaze that had seemed never to leave her face, making her tremble inside.

But no woman—particularly one who had zero actual hands-on experience of men—would consider Vicenzu Trapani husband material. Unlike the rumours about her father's links to organised crime, the stories about him were not just idle gossip. On first impressions alone it was clear he'd earned his flirtatious reputation.

Not that it mattered, she told herself quickly as she skirted around the chattering guests. She had absolutely no intention of falling in love with anyone ever again—and especially not with a man whose behaviour was as provocative as his smile.

All she had to do was ignore her body, and him, for the next couple of hours and concentrate on what really mattered today: Claudia and her new husband.

Plucking a chilled mimosa from a passing waitress, she fixed her gaze on Ciro.

He certainly looked the part. Like his brother, he was tall, dark and handsome, but the resemblance was superficial.

Where Vicenzu was all languid grace and rolled up

shirtsleeves, Ciro wore his suit like custom-built armour, and the imperious tilt of his jaw hinted at an inner confidence and determination that had clearly driven the stratospheric rise of his retail empire.

It was that business success which had persuaded her ultraprotective Sicilian father, Cesare, to agree to the swiftness of this marriage. That and the fact that Ciro came from exactly the kind of respectable background her father craved for his daughters.

The Trapanis were a good, solid Sicilian family, trusted and respected, with a good, solid Sicilian family business to their name. A business that Alessandro Trapani, Ciro's father, had just sold to her father, along with his beautiful home.

Imma felt her shoulders tense. She didn't know all the details of the sale. Despite having groomed her to follow in his footsteps, Cesare was both controlling and secretive about many areas of the business he had built from the ground up.

In his words, old man Trapani had 'got into a mess financially' and wanted a quick sale. Probably it was those same money worries that had led to Alessandro's collapse and tragic, untimely death two months ago.

Her eyes were drawn to the petite woman talking to Claudia. Ribs tightening, she felt an ache of sympathy for her.

With her cloud of dark hair and almond-shaped eyes, Audenzia Trapani must have been exquisite when she was younger, and she was still a beautiful woman. But there was a fragility to her now, and a stillness—as though she was holding herself tightly inside.

Her gaze was still hovering on the older woman when she suddenly became aware that she was being watched.

Looking up, she felt as if her skin had turned inside out. Vicenzu had joined his brother and was staring at her again, his eyes locked on her with an intensity that almost made her flinch.

'Immacolata!'

She turned, relief battling with regret. Her father was bearing down on her, and she felt a familiar rush of love and frustration.

Like a lot of Sicilian men of his generation, Cesare was compact—a solid-bodied barrel of a man. The muscles of his youth were turning heavy now, and yet it would never do to underestimate him on the grounds of age. Cesare was a force of nature. Still handsome, vigorous and uncompromising, a powerful and some thought intimidating presence at any occasion.

'Papà.' She smiled, hoping to deflect the criticism she knew was coming. As he kissed her on each cheek she inhaled the potent mix of cigar smoke and citrusy aftershave that remained in every room he visited long after he'd left.

'Why are you not with your sister?' He frowned. 'Today of all days I want to show both my beautiful daughters off to the world.' His dark eyes softened. 'I know it's hard for you, *piccioncina mia*, watching your sister leave home, and I know you think it's all been too quick, that she's a little young to be married...'

Imma felt her smile tighten, and her father's voice seemed to fade into the hum of background chatter. It wasn't just Claudia's youth that made her feel anxious about the speed of her marriage. It was something more personal: a promise made...

Only neither her father nor her sister wanted to hear her tentative reservations about how fast everything had moved. Cesare had pursued and married their own mother at the age of seventeen, and as for Claudia—she was a dreamer.

And now her dreams of love and a handsome husband and a beautiful home had all come true.

But what about my dreams? Imma flexed her fingers against her cool glass, trying to ignore the pulse of envy beating inside her chest. *When will they come true?*

Hard to say when she actually had no dreams. No idea what she wanted. No idea who she even was.

For her, there had never been any time for thinking about such things. She had always been too busy. Trying to be some kind of mother to Claudia, studying hard at school and then university, and always mindful of the wishes of her father. For without a son to fulfil *his* dreams Cesare had made her the focus of his ambitions.

All his ambitions—including having his say on her choice of future husband, and that was never going to be some local boy made good, like Ciro Trapani, or his rakish older brother.

Not that Vicenzu would ever be interested in her, she thought, her gaze fluttering fleetingly over the perfect angles of his profile. Being in charge of her father's household and a mother figure to Claudia had made her seem far older than her years. And, although she actually shared her sister's shyness, her brief, disappointing interactions with men—she couldn't really call them dates—had left her so wary that she knew her shyness came across as remoteness or disdain.

Hardly qualities that would tempt a man like Vicenzu who, if the internet and the tabloid press were to be believed, was like catnip to women.

But why would she even want to let anyone get close

to her? She was tired of being hurt and humbled. Tired of men running a marathon from her when they realised her surname was Buscetta. Tired of never being good enough, pretty enough, desirable enough for them to face up to her father and fight for the right to be with her.

But her sister's beautiful, romantic wedding was not the time to be letting such thoughts fill her head and, taking a quick, calming breath, she looked up at her father.

'Just at the beginning, Papà.' She took his hand and squeezed it.

Cesare smiled. 'You've been like a mother to her, but marriage is right for Claudia. She doesn't have the temperament for studying or business.'

Imma nodded, her momentary stab of envy instantly swamped by remorse. More than anyone Claudia deserved to be happy, for although their father indulged his youngest daughter, he also found her easy to ignore. Now, though, for the first time in her life, she was in the spotlight.

'I know,' she said quietly.

Cesare grunted. 'She's a homebody and he's a good man for her. Strong, dependable, honest.'

Her father's chest swelled and she could tell he was almost bursting with satisfaction that his daughter had made such a good match socially.

'Come.' He held out his arm. 'Let's go and join your sister—it's nearly time to eat.'

'Where have you been?' It was Claudia, hurrying towards her, clutching the hem of her dress. 'I was just about to send Ciro to find you.'

There was a slight unevenness to her voice, and Imma felt her heart squeeze. She might be a married woman now, but Claudia was still and would always be the little sister she'd comforted whenever she was sad or hurt. Papà was right. Today of all days Imma needed to be there for her—because tomorrow she would be gone.

Pushing back against the ache in her chest, Imma took her sister's hand.

'I just wanted to check in on Corrado,' she said quickly.

Corrado was the Buscettas' Michelin-starred chef, and he had been extremely put out by Cesare's insistence that other Michelin-starred chefs must be flown in at incredible cost from all over the world to help him cater for the wedding breakfast.

But Cesare had been unrepentant. It was his daughter's wedding, and no expense would be spared. He wanted the whole of Sicily—no, make that the whole of Italy—rendered speechless with envy and awe and so, as usual, it had been left to Imma to pour olive oil on troubled waters.

'No, there's nothing wrong,' she added as Ciro and Vicenzu joined them. 'It's just difficult for him, having to share his kitchens, and I didn't want him sulking in any of the photographs.'

'If he does that he'll be looking for a new job,' Cesare growled. 'And he can forget about references. In fact, he can forget about working, full stop. If he doesn't have a smile pinned on his face every second of today I'll make sure he never works again.'

A short, stunned silence followed this explosion. Claudia bit her lip and Ciro looked confused. Vicenzu, on the other hand, seemed more amused than unnerved.

'Of course he won't be looking for another job, Papà,' Imma said firmly. 'Corrado has been with us for ten years. He's one of the family—and we all know how much you value family.'

'And we share those same values, Signor Buscetta.'

Imma glanced sharply over at Vicenzu. For a few half seconds she had been distracted by her father's outburst, but now she felt her stomach swoop down like a kite with a broken tail.

He sounded and looked sincere, and yet she couldn't help thinking he was not. Quickly, in case her father began thinking along the same lines, she said, 'Isn't that how we all ended up here today?'

As she pasted a smile on her face, her father grunted. 'Forgive me. I just want everything to be perfect for my little girl.'

'And it is.' Ciro took a step forward, his deep voice resonating in the space between them. 'If I may, sir, I'd like to thank you for making all this so special for both of us.' He turned to Claudia, who was gazing up at him, her soft brown eyes wide with adoration. 'I promise to make my marriage to Claudia equally memorable.'

Beaming, his good humour restored, Cesare slapped him on the shoulder and then, flicking his ostentatious gold watch free from his cuff, he glanced down at it.

'I'll hold you to that. And now I think we should go and eat. *Ammuninni!*'

Her father held out his arm to Imma, but as she moved to take it Vicenzu sidestepped her, his dark hair flopping over his forehead, his mouth curving into a question mark.

'May I?'

Imma felt her father tense. She knew his opinion of Ciro's older brother. Vicenzu's hedonistic lifestyle and his reputation as a *donnaiolo*—a playboy—had been her father's one and only real objection to Claudia's marriage.

Before she could reply, Cesare said stiffly, 'I think I would prefer to escort my daughter myself.'

There was a short silence, and then her heartbeat accelerated as Vicenzu's teasing dark eyes rested on her face.

'But what would Immacolata prefer?'

Imma froze, his words pinning her to the ground as if he had cast a spell rather than asked a question. Around them the air seemed to turn to stone, and she could sense Claudia's mouth forming an *O* of shock.

No one, certainly not her father, had ever asked about Imma's preferences before, and she had no idea how to respond. But she did know that her father was expecting her to refuse Vicenzu, and maybe it was that assumption, coupled with a sudden longing to indulge in a little impulsive behaviour of her own, that made her turn to Cesare and say calmly, 'I think you should escort Audenzia, Papà. That would be the right and proper thing to do.'

More importantly, it was exactly the right thing for her to say. When he was a young man, her father had just wanted to be rich and powerful, but now what he wanted most was to be accepted in society on an equal footing by people like the Trapanis.

'Of course—you're right,' he said, and Imma felt her heart begin to beat faster as Vicenzu held out his arm.

'Shall we?' he said softly.

Her heart bumping into her ribs, she wondered how he managed to imply so much in two little words. And then, doing her best to ignore the hard swell of his bicep, she followed Claudia and Ciro towards the circus-tent-sized marquee, where the wedding breakfast was being held.

Inside it was impossibly romantic, and Imma felt her stomach flip over as Vicenzu led her to their flower-strewn table. She was already regretting defying her father. Vicenzu Trapani probably flirted in his sleep and she needed to remember that—not let the emotion of the day or his dark eyes suggest anything different.

'So, Vicenzu,' she said quickly, before he had a chance to speak, 'I've heard so much about your hotel. Tell me…how many people work at La Dolce Vita?'

Dropping down next to her, he frowned. 'Well, Immacolata, that's a tricky one. Let me see… I guess, on a good day, probably about forty percent of them.'

The smile tugging at his mouth was impossible to resist, and of their own accord her lips started to curl upward, like the sun rising in the morning sky.

'I know—you think they should all be working. And you're right. I need to crack the whip a bit.'

As his smile slowly unfurled, she felt her stomach flicker like a flame in a breeze. 'I meant—' she began.

He was grinning now. 'I'm just teasing. The answer is I don't know or care. All I know is I get to enjoy your company for the foreseeable future. And, as you're the most beautiful woman in this tiny, unassuming tent…' he glanced mockingly around the vast marquee '…that makes me the luckiest man on earth.'

A cool shiver ran over her skin. Her heart was suddenly beating so fast she felt it might burst free of her ribs.

'Really?' She met his gaze calmly, even as his words resounded inside her head.

'Really. Truly. Absolutely. Unequivocally. Did I say that right?'

She saw his eyes light up as she smiled. 'Yes, only that doesn't make it true.'

'But why would I lie?'

His tone was still playful, but he was staring at her intently.

'Look, I'm not good for much—just ask anyone who knows me...'

He leaned forward so that he was filling her view, and she felt her skin grow hot and tight as he stared down at her steadily.

'But I am a connoisseur of beauty, and you are a very beautiful woman.'

For a second or three the world seemed to stop—or at least the hubbub in the tent faded to a dull hum beneath the uneven thump of her heartbeat. He probably said that to every woman he met, and yet she couldn't stop herself from hoping that he was telling the truth.

He took her hand and she felt her stomach flutter. But he didn't kiss it. Instead he turned her arm over and examined the skin on her wrist.

'What are you doing?' she asked.

'Looking for chinks in your armour,' he murmured.

There was a brief shifting silence, and then he glanced up as waiters began filing into the marquee.

'Great—it's time to eat.'

His eyes met hers, soft and yet intense in a way that made her breathing knot.

'Let's hope the food is as delectable as my hostess,' he said. 'I don't think I've ever been hungrier...'

The food had been incredible. Seven courses accompanied by a note-perfect string quartet. Then there had been speeches, and now Claudia was leaning into Cesare as they slowly circled in the traditional father-and-daughter dance.

But Imma had barely registered any of it. Not the food, nor the music or the toasts. Of course she had gone through the pantomime of raising her glass to her mouth and smiling and nodding, but inside she had been too busy trying to work out the enigma that was Vicenzu Trapani.

She'd expected to like him—*obviously*. A man didn't get the kind of reputation he had for no reason. And this must be how he was with every woman. She was no different in her response to his easy charm and lush beauty.

And yet although she had wanted to find him shallow and spoilt, flirtatious and flippant—and he was all of those things—she felt she might have misjudged him.

Particularly in those moments like now, when he seemed to forget that she was there and his eyes would seek out his mother at the far end of the table.

Her breathing lost its rhythm. Of course she missed her own mother, but his loss was so recent…still raw.

Glancing over at him, she said hesitantly, 'It must be difficult.'

'Difficult?' He raised one perfect eyebrow.

'Today. I mean, without your father. I know Papà wishes he'd come to him sooner.'

Vicenzu's handsome face didn't change, but she could sense an immediate tightening beneath the surface of his skin.

'It's no harder than any other day.'

The lazy amusement had left his voice and her cheeks grew warm. Wanting to kick herself, she glanced across the dance floor to where Ciro had taken over from Cesare. Watching him gaze down into Claudia's upturned face, she felt an ache of the loss to come.

'I'm sorry, Vicenzu—'

'It's Vicè—and, no, *I'm* sorry.' He frowned, his face creasing without impairing its beauty. 'You're right. It is hard without him, and I should have expected it to be, but I'm an idiot.'

Maybe it was the bleakness in his eyes, or perhaps his earlier defiance of her father, but she felt suddenly protective of him.

'You're not an idiot for missing your father. I miss my mother every day.'

They were so close she could feel his warm breath on her face, see the stubble already forming on his jaw. For a full sixty seconds they stared at each other, wide-eyed, mesmerised by the bond they seemed to have formed out of nowhere, and then, standing up, he held out his hand.

'Maybe not,' he said slowly. 'But I will be an idiot if I leave this wedding without having at least one dance with you.' He hesitated. 'That is if you'll dance with me?'

Her mouth felt dry and her blood was humming in her ears. She could feel a hundred pairs of eyes on her. But her eyes were fixed on his and, nodding slowly, she stood up and took his hand.

CHAPTER TWO

BREATHING OUT, VICÈ pulled Imma against him, keeping his beautiful face blank of expression. It was all part of the plan, he told himself. The first step in his great seduction of Immacolata Buscetta.

But inside his head a war was raging between the man he was and the man he was trying to be and needed to be.

No change there, then, he thought irritably.

Except this time there would be no second chances.

It should be easy—and had it been any other woman it would have been. Women liked him. He liked them. But Imma wasn't like other women. She was the daughter of his enemy—and as such he'd expected to hate her on sight.

Everything he'd seen and heard about her in advance had made that seem likely. He'd expected her to be cool and reserved, less overtly aggressive than Cesare, but still her father's daughter. And she was definitely a princess. Watching her with her staff, it had been clear to him that her quiet words and the decisive up-tilt to her jaw held the same authority as a royal command.

Her dark, demure dress seemed to confirm the message that she wanted to be taken seriously—only it couldn't hide her long, coltish legs.

He felt his chest rise and fall.

And as for that long dark hair… It might be neatly knotted at the nape of her neck but he could all too easily imagine running his fingers through its rich, silky length, and her bee-stung parted lips definitely seemed to contradict the wariness in her green eyes.

In short, she was beautiful. Just not the cold, diamond-hard beauty he'd anticipated.

And that was the problem.

He'd wanted to go in for the kill—do it quickly and cleanly like a shark—only it was turning out to be so much harder than he'd anticipated. Particularly with Imma's smooth, supple body pressed against his.

His chest tightened and, catching sight of his mother's face again, he closed his eyes, wishing it was as easy to shut out the confusion he felt on the inside.

Could he do this? Could he actually pull this off?

They were the questions he'd been asking himself for weeks now—ever since he and Ciro had sat in that bar drinking bourbon.

Ciro was his brother and his best friend. There was less than a year between their birthdays, so he couldn't remember a time when Ciro had been smaller, weaker, slower than him.

Maybe he never had been.

It had certainly felt that way for most of his life.

Opening his eyes, he watched his brother dance past, his hand wrapped around Claudia's waist, his face gazing down into hers.

He looked every inch the devoted husband—and he would look that way right up until the moment when he told his new wife the truth and her world came tumbling down.

And, even though he would have preferred to take things more slowly, when the time came he would do the same to Imma. He wanted vengeance every bit as much as Ciro.

His heart stilled.

His father had not been a critical or judgemental man, but he remembered once as a child they had been in Palermo, and a stocky man with a sneering smile had got out of a car and Alessandro's eyes had narrowed.

Sensing his son's curiosity, his father had told him he was a man 'without honour'. He had never forgotten the man's name or his father's words. Coming from his mild, gentle father, they had shocked him.

Now they choked him.

Cesare Buscetta had hounded and humbled Alessandro to death. He needed to pay for his crimes, and it was Vicenzu's job—*his duty*—to make that happen.

'Excuse me, Imma…'

It was Ciro, a small apologetic smile playing around his mouth. His eyes met momentarily with his brother's.

'It's time for Claudia to go and change, and apparently you said you would help her—'

Imma was frowning, and she seemed dazed—almost as though she'd been woken from a dream. 'I'm so sorry… of course I did. Would you mind?'

'Vicè?' His brother frowned too. 'Imma's talking to you.'

'Yeah, I heard, bro.' Feeling Ciro's gaze on his face, he softened his voice and stared down at Imma until he saw a flush colour her cheeks. 'I mind tremendously, but I'll forgive you as long as you come right back.'

As she lifted her face and looked up at him his chest tightened painfully. He'd sworn an oath with Ciro and he was going to keep it—but it would be so much easier if she had eyes of a different colour.

Watching her walk away, he gritted his teeth.

It wasn't fair. Why did her eyes have to be *green*? And not just green but the exact lush green of the No-cellara olives that grew so abundantly on his family's estate. Olives he had helped pick as a child. Olives his father had nurtured and loved almost as much as he had nurtured and loved his family.

It was one of his earliest memories—that first time he'd been allowed to join his father and the other estate workers for the harvest.

He had been so proud when he'd shown his father his haul, and Alessandro had not so much as hinted that the fruit he'd picked was too small and not ripe enough.

It had been that way for his entire life—his father covering up his mistakes, never holding him accountable, always giving him another chance. He couldn't even pinpoint when it had first started.

Had it been at school? When he'd got into trouble for trading tips on how to kiss girls in exchange for getting his homework done? Or when he'd got drunk and driven a tractor around the olive groves? He'd written off the tractor, and some of the estate's oldest trees—but, just like on all the other occasions when he'd messed up, Alessandro had simply sighed and shaken his head.

Something bitter rose in his throat—the burning anger that had been swirling inside his chest since his mother's distraught phone call.

If only his father had told him the truth about Buscetta he would have been able to help. It could have been his chance to make amends. It wasn't as if he was still a child. He didn't need protecting from the truth.

And then, just like that, he felt his anger drain away swiftly, like water spiralling down a plughole.

To his father he had still needed protecting.

That was why Alessandro had kept both his financial and his health worries to himself. Vicenzu glanced over at his brother. And that was why Ciro was so insistent that they seek revenge on Buscetta.

Unlike him, his brother had always been independently successful on a scale that far surpassed their father, and the idea that Alessandro hadn't thought Ciro man enough to take on his father's problems had incensed his younger brother.

The truth was actually the opposite, he thought numbly. His father had known that he'd be able to rely on Ciro, but he hadn't wanted to confide in one son and not the other, so he'd sacrificed himself so that *he*, Vicenzu, wouldn't feel inadequate.

It was yet another reason for him to feel guilty.

'How's it going?'

Glancing up at his brother, he shrugged. 'It's going fine, I think.' He leaned forward and picked up a *confetti* from a nearby table. It was a traditional gift for the wedding guests. His mother still had hers from her own wedding. Five pastel-coloured sugared almonds—a reminder that married life was both sweet and bitter—and five wishes for the new husband and wife.

Health, wealth, happiness, children and a long life.

His shoulders tensed. Now, thanks to Buscetta, his parents' wishes had withered like olives exposed to a hard frost.

He sensed Ciro's impatience even before he heard it in his voice. 'You *think*? What does that mean?'

He felt a flicker of irritation—and envy. Ever since he could remember people had wanted to make his life easy. Not just his parents, but his friends and pretty much every woman he met. Ciro too. Until now. Now his brother was so on edge, so picky and demanding all the time.

But Claudia had always been the easier sister to seduce. She was younger, naive in the extreme, and had clearly been groomed for marriage. All Ciro had had to do was get past her monstrous father. Okay, that had sounded tough on paper, but in reality Cesare had laid out the red carpet for him.

Obviously.

His brother ticked all the boxes, whereas Vicenzu just owned a hotel. It might be the most celebrated hotel in the Western hemisphere—part sanctuary, part crash pad for its hard-partying, glamorous A-list clientele— but still…

And, of course, there was his reputation—

'Vicè!' His brother's voice tugged him back into the present. 'I thought seduction was supposed to be your area of expertise?'

'It is.' He turned towards his brother, his hands itching to both hit him and hug him. As usual, he went down the path of least resistance. '*Scialla*—just chill, Ciro, okay?' Grabbing his brother by the shoulders, he pulled him into an embrace. '*Festina lente*, bro.'

'There's no time for chilling, *bro*,' his brother said irritably. 'And quoting Latin at me doesn't change the facts. We agreed—you agreed—'

'Yeah, and I'm doing it.'

'Do it faster.' They were facing each other and their eyes met. 'I don't want to be stuck in this marriage for any longer than I have to be.'

'I know.'

Ciro held his gaze. 'Look, ever since I was a teenager I've watched women climb over each other to get to you. Immacolata Buscetta will be exactly the same. So just do this for Mamma, and for Papà, and then everything will go back to how it was before.'

Except it wouldn't.

They would have avenged their father, but nothing could bring him back to life. They would have the business and their home, but their mother still wouldn't have her husband.

He glanced over to where Audenzia was sitting, sipping coffee. His parents had been so devoted to each other they had never spent a night apart during their forty years of marriage. He'd always feared falling short of their ideal, and now he was having to seduce a woman he hated into marrying him.

'I can't help feeling that Papà wouldn't like this,' he said quietly.

Ciro stared at him. 'Maybe not—but he's not here to ask, is he? And if you're having second thoughts, maybe you should ask yourself why that's the case.'

The pain was sharp and humbling. And just what Vicenzu needed to clear the confusion from his mind.

He had made and broken enough promises in his life.

This time he would do whatever it took to keep one.

It was dark when Ciro and Claudia finally left.

'He will take care of her, won't he?'

Vicè was standing next to Imma at the edge of the

marquee. Having waved off the happy couple, most of the guests had already gone back inside, but she had wanted to wait until the car had disappeared.

He felt a rush of anticipation—like that moment on a rollercoaster ride just before the track dropped down. Now that it was close, he just wanted to make it happen.

'Yes, of course,' he lied.

She nodded. 'You don't have to wait with me,' she said, glancing back at the distant car, her green eyes tracking its progress. 'I know it's silly, but it's the first time she's gone away without me.'

'I want to wait.' He hesitated. 'And there's nowhere I'd rather be than here.' Taking her hand, he gently pulled her closer. 'With you.'

Her eyes lifted to his face, and there was a faint frown on her brow as she tugged her pashmina closer to her body. He felt his blood start to hum. He'd bet his last sugared almond that she was trying to hide how aroused she was by his words.

'I don't think we know each other well enough for you to say that,' she said quietly.

'So let's get to know each other better.' He took a deep breath. 'Let's go somewhere more private.'

She looked up at him, her green eyes wide with confusion and a curiosity that made his groin turn to stone.

He nodded. 'I know it's sudden, and I'm guessing you think I do this kind of thing all the time. But I don't. Usually I'm just looking for fun—but not today. Not with you.'

She bit her lip, and for a moment he thought he'd gone too far, too fast.

'Look, forget it,' he said quickly. 'I must be crazy, suggesting something like that—'

She nodded slowly. 'Yes, you are.'

He felt her fingers tighten around his.

'But maybe it's about time I did something crazy too.'

His heart gave a leap, and he felt shock mingling with confusion. He couldn't believe she was agreeing with him.

'I should say goodbye to Papà first—'

'No.' He squeezed her hand. 'Don't go back in— please.' There was no way he was going to let her talk to Buscetta before she left. 'My driver's out front. We can call your father on our way to the airport.'

She stared at him for a moment, and then she smiled. 'Or we could go completely crazy and take my father's helicopter...'

Leaning back into the cream leather upholstery, Vicè breathed out slowly. The Buscetta helicopter was rising up into the dark sky, its rotor blades whipping up the discarded *coriandoli* so that for a moment he felt as if he were in a snow globe—a sensation exacerbated by the feeling of his world being turned upside down and shaken vigorously.

He could hardly believe it.

That Imma had agreed to his impulsive suggestion that they get to know one another seemed fantastical enough, but for her to more or less commandeer her father's helicopter in order to make their escape seemed too preposterous to be true.

And yet that was exactly what was happening.

At that moment Imma turned and smiled at him, her eyes bright with eagerness and pleasure at her part in the adventure, and he felt his heart jump, his body responding to her sudden and thrilling abandonment of the normal expected preliminaries.

Well, perhaps not all of them.

Remembering that this was supposed to be a seduction, he lifted her hand to his mouth, feeling her pulse dart under the skin like a minnow in a pond.

'Will this thing make it to the mainland?' he asked softly.

'The mainland?' she repeated.

He held her gaze, his eyebrow curving upward at the question in her voice.

He and Ciro had accepted that Buscetta would never countenance Vicenzu courting Imma. Plus, the second brother falling in love with his other daughter was so implausible it would almost certainly hint at some kind of plot, so they'd decided that it would be better to present him with a fait accompli.

His shoulders stiffened. Of course before he'd even thought about how he was going to make that happen Ciro, being Ciro, had already proposed to Claudia and started the process of arranging the paperwork for their marriage.

But seducing a woman was not something Vicè consciously did—normally it just happened. He had no idea how to cold-bloodedly reproduce that organic process, so he'd left it to the last minute—like he did everything else in his life.

Not that he'd told his uber-efficient brother that.

Arriving at the wedding, he'd decided to seduce Imma and then use his reputation as leverage for their marriage. It would be a delicate balancing act. She'd know he wouldn't be Cesare's choice for her husband. But nor would her father want her to be viewed as just another notch on Vicenzu's bedpost. And obviously his plan wouldn't work if they kept their liaison private, which was why he needed it to play out in public.

And where better to find maximum publicity than at his celebrity-studded hotel with its inbuilt entourage of photographers?

'I thought I was taking you back to mine,' he said.

'To the Dolce Vita?' She looked confused. 'I thought you wanted to go somewhere private.'

Good point, he thought, his shoulders tensing.

It was a rookie error—except he wasn't a rookie. As Ciro had so pointedly remarked earlier, this was supposed to be his area of expertise.

Glancing out of the window, he felt his pulse slow as he realised he'd made another error in assuming he was calling the shots. Imma might not be planning to go back to his hotel, but they were clearly not just flying in circles so...

'I do,' he said. He let his gaze linger on her face. 'And I should have realised that totally rules out my hotel. But ever since you walked into that church behind your sister I haven't been able to think straight.'

Watching her chew at her lip, he felt his heart kick against his ribs.

'I'm guessing you have somewhere in mind,' he said softly.

He felt her fingers move against his and, glancing down, was almost shocked to see her hand entwined with his. Holding hands was not his thing, but his parents had always done it and his ribs tightened as he pictured his mother sitting alone at the wedding. That was another crime to chalk up to Cesare Buscetta's relentless greed.

But as he felt the ever-present trickle of anger start to rise and swell he pushed the memory away. His anger would wait. Right now he needed to focus on the task in hand.

Closing his grip around her fingers, he gently pulled her closer. 'So where are you taking me?'

No doubt Imma had some favourite boutique hotel in mind—somewhere quiet, intimate—and actually that might work for him. They could lie low until he had her eating out of his hand, and then he could discreetly tip off the paparazzi.

He felt her gaze on his face.

'Papà has a villa on Pantelleria...'

Pantelleria. Unlike most people in the world, he'd heard of the island—but, like most of the population, he'd never set foot on it. Why would he? It was basically a black volcanic speck in the Mediterranean between Sicily and Tunisia.

'Right...' He nodded, holding his easy smile in place. 'Your father isn't going to have a problem with that?'

She hesitated, her face tensing a little as though she was weighing up what to say next.

'He bought it as a kind of hideaway, somewhere to get away from work—only he's not very good about handing over the reins, so he never really goes there. But Claudia and I love it. It's just so beautiful—and very private.'

Her eyes seemed to grow even more opaque.

'But if you've changed your mind I can get Marco to—'

She was close enough that he could feel her small, firm breasts through the thin fabric of his shirt, and the tiny shivers of anticipation scampering over her skin. Seducing Imma at a hideaway on a remote island owned by Buscetta himself was about as far away from ideal as it could get, but he didn't want to jeopardise this mood of intimacy between them.

The time for talking was over.

He looked down at the pulse beating erratically at the base of her beautiful throat, feeling his body harden to stone for the second time in as many minutes. Reaching up, he caught her chin with his hand, tilting her face to his. 'Nothing's changed.'

He could make it work—he *would* make it work.

Needing to defuse any indecision she might still be feeling, he did the first thing that came into his head. Lowering his mouth to hers, he kissed her.

Whatever he'd been expecting when his lips touched hers, it wasn't what actually happened. For a brief second or two she stilled against him, her mouth softening beneath his, lips parting on an intake of breath, and then her hand slid over his neck, fingers pressing lightly against his skin as though she was reading Braille.

Barely breathing, he moved his lips over hers, teasing her with the whispering heat of his mouth, the firm tip of his tongue, stirring her senses, tasting her, all the while telling himself that he hated this woman, that she was guilty by association.

But then she moaned softly, shifting against him. Her fingers curled through his hair to grasp his skull, her tongue pushing between his lips, and hunger, hot and powerful, punched him in the gut.

Her scent enveloped him and, breathing in sharply, he made a rough, incoherent sound against her mouth, trying and failing to still the blood pounding through his veins, almost idiotically stupefied by the strength of his desire and hers.

He was hard—very hard—and, framing her face

with his hands, he kissed her fiercely, pulling her closer
so that she pressed against him, wanting more of her,
needing more of her—

'Miss Buscetta?'

Imma jerked back and they stared at one another
dazedly as the pilot's voice filled the cabin.

'We'll be coming in to land in about five minutes. There
might be a few crosswinds, but nothing to worry about.'

With a hand that trembled slightly, Imma pressed
the intercom. 'Thank you, Marco.'

Vicenzu breathed out unsteadily, blindsided by her
response, and utterly floored by his own.

He had wanted so much more than just her mouth.
And, judging by the dull ache in his groin, he still did.

His heart beating out of time, he struggled to pull
his brain back online. 'Imma—'

Her green eyes fluttered to his face, wide and startled. The curves of her cheeks were flushed with desire,
or embarrassment, or maybe both.

He swore inwardly. 'I'm sorry. I didn't expect—I
didn't mean for that to happen—'

Actually, what he hadn't expected was for it to feel
like that—for her to be so gloriously responsive, so fierce,
so sweet, so everything he'd ever wanted in a woman.

But how was that possible?

He was only supposed to be seducing this woman
to avenge his family.

'I understand.'

She inched backwards, slipping her hand free of his.
He watched her fold it back into her lap, his heart beating as violently as if he'd just sprinted for a finishing
line. Only for once—incredibly—he didn't appear to
be on the winner's podium.

'Imma—'

'Please.' She held up her hand and her beautiful mouth no longer looked soft and kissable but pinched, as though she was trying to hold something in. 'I don't need to hear it.'

'Hear what?'

Her face was pale and set, and there was a tension to her body he recognised. It was as though she was bracing herself for bad news.

'I've heard it all before,' she said, staring past him. 'Let me guess. You're worried things are moving too fast. Or maybe you respect me too much? That's always popular.'

He frowned. Her words made no sense. 'I don't understand—'

She ignored him. 'You know, back at the wedding I thought you were different. But I guess when it comes to the crunch you're just like everyone else.'

The bitterness in her voice was unmistakable now.

'I'm sorry for taking up so much of your time, Signor Trapani. But don't worry. You can go back to your precious hotel and the rest of your "sweet life" now. Just tell Marco where you need to go and he'll take you.'

There was a slight judder as the helicopter touched down, and before he had a chance to respond, even to absorb her words, she'd pulled off her seat belt and was out of the door and gone.

He stared after her, shock and outrage swirling up inside him, and then he was wrenching himself free and following her into the warm night air. She was moving fast, and he found himself having to run to catch up with her.

He'd never run after a woman metaphorically, let

alone in reality, and the fact that he was having to do so made his irritation intensify with every step.

'Imma!'

She carried on walking and, frustrated by the sight of the smooth, untroubled knot at the nape of her neck, he caught her arm, jerking her round to face him.

'Where's all this coming from? All I said was—'

Her eyes narrowed and she shook his hand off. 'I heard you the first time.'

Watching the bow of her mouth tremble, Vicè felt his breath hitch in his throat. Before her anger had been crimped, confined by a forced politeness, now she was clearly furious.

'Look, I get it. It was a wedding. You were bored, or curious—maybe both. But I do have feelings and I am done with being picked up and dropped like some toy.'

She glared at him, her hands curling into fists. 'But I suppose I should be thankful that at least one Trapani brother has the courage of his convictions.'

His jaw clenched. Being compared unfavourably to Ciro was such a frequent occurrence he rarely even reacted any more, but Imma's criticism, delivered in that clipped, dismissive manner, somehow got under his skin, so that suddenly he was having to rein in his temper, usually so slow to rise.

'Meaning?' he said.

Her lip curled with contempt. 'I mean, unlike you, Ciro's not scared of my father.'

Listening to her words echo in the silence, Imma felt slightly sick.

She hadn't meant to say that out loud, only there was no real point in continuing with this farce.

Vicenzu Trapani was a beautiful liar, and she was an unforgivable idiot.

What was worse, for just a few short hours she had actually started to hope…started to think that Vicè was different—that, incredibly, like Claudia, she had met a man who was prepared to stand proudly beside her.

And not just any man—a man who was in a class of his own. Cool, glamorous, and with a smile that made her body ache and a mouth that turned her inside out.

Remembering her uninhibited response to his kiss, she felt her skin grow warm. She had kissed men before—three, to be precise—but Vicè's kiss had been like nothing she'd ever experienced, and if Marco's disembodied voice hadn't interrupted she would have gone on kissing him forever.

Her cheeks burned as she replayed that sound she'd made when he'd pulled her against his hard body. It had felt so good, so right—but clearly not good or right enough for him to want to continue.

She hung on to her temper as he took a step towards her, his eyes narrowing like chips of volcanic rock.

'*Scared?* Of your *father*? Let me tell you something, Imma. I feel many things for your father, but fear isn't one of them. I'm no more scared of him than Ciro is.'

Gone was the handsome easy-going playboy. The skin across his cheekbones was tight, like a ship's sail in a strong wind. But it was the rawness in his voice that convinced her that he was telling the truth.

And just like that her own anger turned to air.

'I thought you'd changed your mind.' She swallowed. 'Like all the others.'

There was a beat of silence and she heard him breathe out unsteadily.

'I panicked,' he said.

His dark eyes found hers, and the naked heat in them sent a jolt through her body.

'But not because I wanted to back out. I thought I'd come on too strong.' He hesitated, and then, reaching out, took her hand and pulled her closer. 'I meant what I said earlier. I want to get to know you better.'

As he gazed down at her she felt her pulse begin to beat a little faster.

'And if you still want that too then I won't let anything or anyone—including your father—get in the way of that happening. Do you understand?'

Her heart was pressing against her ribs. It was what she'd wanted to hear for so long—and, more importantly, it was clear he meant it.

Nodding slowly, she let him pull her into his arms.

CHAPTER THREE

'So, WHO ARE these "others"?'

Glancing up at Vicè, Imma frowned. Neither of them was hungry, but they were drinking wine on the vast terrace next to the pool. Or rather he was drinking. She was too jittery to do anything but clutch the stem of her glass. Besides, just looking at him made her tongue stick to the roof of her mouth.

Watching him languidly stretch out his long legs, she felt knots form in her stomach. He was so perfect, with his dark poet's eyes and panther-like grace...

Trying to stay calm, she gazed past him. It was a bad idea. Somebody—probably Marianna, the housekeeper—had lit some candles, and the twitching flames made the curves of his face even more dangerously appealing.

Accompanying the darkness was the lightest of breezes—a whisper of dry air from Africa—and on it came the scent of the roses and jasmine that Marianna cherished in the garden that surrounded the villa on all sides.

The undiluted romance of it all sent a tremor through her blood.

She cleared her throat. 'Others?'

He picked up his wine glass, lounging back in his

seat, his dark eyes roaming her face. 'Earlier, you said something about me changing my mind "like the others".'

'Oh, that…' She felt a prickle spread over her skin and down her spine. 'It's nothing, really.'

How could someone like him truly understand? But he held her gaze.

She sighed. 'Just that my dates were always ever so keen on me—until they worked out who my father was. And then—'

'Oh, I see,' he said softly.

She nodded. 'Papà has a reputation. Friends in low places. I'm sure you've read the stories about him?'

He shook his head, his eyes gleaming. 'Too busy reading about myself.'

The teasing note in his voice made her skin sting. Pulse quickening, she glanced away. What was he thinking when he looked at her like that? And why did her body like it so much?

Reaching across the table, he took her hand. 'Look, what they can't find out they make up. It's not important.'

His voice was gentle but his dark eyes were burning into her, the intensity of their focus accelerating her already racing pulse. He was everything she wanted, but everything she feared. Compelling. Confident. Curious about her.

She had never talked like this to anyone. Her father's moods were too changeable and Claudia was so young and innocent.

She felt his fingers tighten around hers.

'Those men had no right to judge you, *cara*.' His beautiful mouth twisted. 'Believe me, I know. People think because they read about you that they know you, but they don't.' His eyes met hers. 'They really don't.'

Remembering the stories she'd read about him, she felt a twinge of guilt. How could she complain about being judged when she was guilty of doing the same to him?

'And those people don't know you,' she said, her words tumbling over themselves. 'The real you. You're funny, and smart, and kind, and sweet…'

Her voice petered out. Beside her, Vicè leaned back a little, his expression midway between surprise and amusement—unsurprising, given that she'd sounded like some teenage fangirl.

Cringing inwardly, she frowned. 'Look, maybe this wasn't such a good idea. I'll get Marco to drop you back to your hotel—'

Reaching over, he tugged her towards him. Then he smiled…a slow, flickering smile like a candle being lit that made a pulse of excitement beat beneath her skin.

'*Cara*, forget about my hotel…you're the sweetness in my life.'

Oh, she liked him so much—and she'd almost ruined everything with her stupid accusations. But this was all so new and different. She was different with him. More impulsive and open. Bolder.

Her body tensed. Only not so bold that she was looking forward to facing her father.

Picturing Cesare's outburst, she shivered. He would be angry enough about her leaving the wedding early, but his fury would be visible from space when he found out she had left with Vicè and come here. Particularly as he'd hinted that he was finally ready to talk about her role at Trapani.

'How mad is he going to be?'

Her chin jerked up. 'How did you know what I was thinking?'

'Just a guess.' He sighed. 'Come on, let's go inside. I think you need something stronger than wine.'

Inside, he poured two glasses of grappa and, dropping down beside her on the sofa, handed her one. 'Look, I feel like this is my fault. Why don't I call him? Explain—'

'No, absolutely not.' She shook her head. She could think of nothing that would antagonise Cesare more.

Leaning forward, Vicè stroked the curve of her cheekbone with a tenderness that made her skin melt.

'I'm not scared of him, Imma.' His face stilled as though something had just occurred to him. 'Are *you*?'

She shook her head. 'Of course not. Papà just doesn't like surprises. He has plans for me. Expectations. Your father's business—he wants me to run it.'

He lifted his glass. 'And you don't want to.'

It was a statement, not a question. And just for a moment his eyes seemed to narrow. But when he lowered his glass she realised he was just curious.

'Yes, I do. It's a wonderful business. And it's the least I can do for Papà. I want to be there for him.'

Her pulse skipped. Her father was going to be apoplectic, but it was the aftermath of his rage she was dreading.

He would become even more controlling—particularly regarding her matrimonial choices. Claudia could have her Ciro, but Cesare wanted Imma to marry well—and by 'well' he meant to a man nearer his own age, whose wealth was equal to the GDP of some small country.

Love hadn't been mentioned.

She shivered inside. She couldn't disappoint her father. He needed her to fulfil his dreams.

All she wanted was just one night for herself.

An experience that was hers and hers alone.

An experience she would remember forever—an encounter that would imprint on her body and mind to help her through years of dutiful marriage to a man she didn't love.

Tonight she wanted fire and ecstasy. She wanted to understand her own needs and desires...be in charge of making that small but important change from sheltered, uninformed virgin to a woman who had experienced the storm of passion.

Picking up her glass, she saw her hand was shaking a little. Her body was humming...fear mingling with desire. Fear of missing out. Fear of giving in to what she wanted.

And she wanted Vicè.

Her hunger, her need for him, was like a tornado inside her, upturning everything in its path so that her skin could barely hold it in.

And by bringing Vicè here she had already sealed her fate. Her father was going to come down on her hard and fast. So shouldn't she make sure it was for something that mattered?

And what mattered more than choosing your first lover?

This might be her last opportunity to make that choice and she was choosing Vicè. Because he was handsome, charming, and most importantly she trusted him.

'But I want to be here with you too,' she said slowly. 'And I don't care how angry that makes him.'

Their gazes locked.

'He has no reason to be angry.'

His dark eyes held her fast and heat shivered down her spine.

'Nothing's happened.'

Something stirred deep inside her, and she took a steadying breath.

'Nothing's happened *yet*,' she said softly.

Her hunger for him was like the lick of a flame. Only he could put out the fire.

The glass in her hand was shaking. Reaching over, he took it from her.

'Are you saying you want something to happen?' he asked.

His eyes were steady on her face, his expression intent, as though he was trying to read her mind.

She didn't know where to start, or how to ask for what she wanted. But she knew that she wanted to share it, feel it, with him—with this man. With Vicè.

She nodded. 'Yes, that is what I'm saying.'

Her belly clenched. She sounded so formal, so uptight, but she couldn't help it. Her body was just so wound up, so hot and tight with hope and need and anticipation. And fear of rejection.

Her stomach was a ball of nerves. 'It's just that I'm scared—'

'Of being hurt?' He gave her a crooked smile. 'It's a risk, and I guess it's a particularly big risk with someone like me…someone with my history.' His dark, mocking face was suddenly serious. 'But if it makes you feel better I think I'm the one in danger here. You make me feel things I've never felt, want things I've never wanted before—'

Heat surged over her skin, lifting the hairs on her

arms, making her breasts tingle and tighten. So many choices had been made for her already. So much decided and dictated. This night with Vicè would be hers, and hers alone.

'I want them too,' she whispered. 'I want you.'

But he was gorgeous and sexy, and he had his pick of beautiful, experienced women. Would he really want someone so inexpert and gauche?

For a moment she thought about telling him the truth. Only what if it changed things between them?

Vicè might be a playboy, but he was also a Sicilian. What if beneath the languid posturing he retained an old-school Sicilian attitude to taking a woman's virginity? What if he backed off?

She made up her mind.

Being here with him was straight out of a fantasy, and raising the topic of her virginity would introduce a cool reality she wasn't ready to face yet.

'Shall we go somewhere even more private?' she said softly. 'More intimate...'

Vicenzu stared at her in silence, a pulse beating in his throat, her voice replaying inside his head.

Intimate.

He felt his belly flip over.

Intimate.

The word brushed against his skin. It made him think of subdued lighting, soft laughter and naked bodies.

His own body turned to granite as she bit her lip.

'Imma, are you sure?' Holding her gaze, he softened his voice. 'I know my reputation, and I don't want you to think that's why I'm here.'

She shook her head. 'I don't think that.'

She was staring up at him, her face expressionless, but he could hear the nervous edge in her voice and knew she was trying to sound calmer than she felt.

It was understandable. Given how protective Buscetta was about his daughters, it was unlikely she did this kind of thing very often—and certainly not under her over-controlling father's nose. Clearly being here, in her father's lair, was spooking her.

Her cheeks were flushed and her dark hair was coming undone from the knot at her neck. He studied her face, lost momentarily in the delicacy of her features and the flame in her eyes. He felt his pulse accelerate. He could do this, but he needed to take charge, keep it light—not let her beauty get in the way of what was really happening here.

'I'm happy to wait, *cara*. Well, maybe happy is pushing it.' He grimaced. 'Obviously I'd be in a lot of pain—'

She laughed then, and for a moment he almost forgot why he was there. It was such a lovely sound. All he could think about was how to make her laugh again.

But then he blanked his mind as she stood up, pulling him to his feet.

'I might just freshen up.'

She seemed more nervous now they were in her bedroom, and he kissed her softly on the mouth.

'Good idea. I'll wait here. Take all the time you need.'

Actually, he was the one fighting for time. He needed to put some distance between himself and Imma otherwise...

As the door closed he began unbuttoning his shirt,

and then, frowning, he pulled out his wallet. He was checking he had condoms when he noticed he had a notification on his phone. It was a voicemail from Ciro.

'Vicenzu, it's me... Look, I can't do this for much longer. I've fulfilled my part. She's going to sign the house over to me today. You need to get your side done, and quickly. Whatever it takes to get the business back, do it. Because I don't know how much longer I can keep the pretence up.'

He thought about the edge to Imma's voice.

Then he pictured his mother sitting alone at the wedding.

Taking back his father's business and their family home would go a long way towards making her smile again. And it would wipe the smile off Buscetta's face at the same time.

He knew what his mother would say. That two wrongs didn't make a right.

His jaw tightened. No, they didn't. On this occasion two wrongs would make two rights.

Hearing the door to the bathroom open, he texted Ciro quickly, then tossed his phone onto a chair. Composing his face, he looked up—and his breath stalled in his throat.

Imma was standing in the doorway, her long dark hair hanging loose over her shoulders.

Her naked shoulders.

Actually, she was entirely naked except for a tiny pair of cream lace panties—a fact that his groin had apparently registered several moments before his eyes.

His body hardening to stone, he stood hypnotised by her small rounded breasts and rose-coloured nipples. Her skin was the colour of the purest cold-pressed virgin olive oil, and just looking at it made his ribcage tighten around his chest.

He was used to nudity, and blasé about beauty, but there was a vulnerability to her pose that had everything and nothing to do with sex.

His pact with Ciro was forgotten. And his anger and grief and guilt—everything that had propelled him to this softly lit room—was swept away by a need he had never experienced before.

He stared at her, dry-mouthed, feeling the blood throb through his body.

She took a step forward, reaching out to touch him.

'Wait,' he said gently. 'Let me look at you first.'

She looked up at him, and he took his time absorbing her beauty.

Expression shuttered, he stepped closer and stroked the curve of her cheek. 'Don't be shy. You're beautiful.'

'So are you.'

Heat flared inside him as she touched his chest, her warm fingers sending shock waves over his skin. Leaning forward, he brushed his mouth lightly over hers, sliding his hand through her hair.

It wasn't a kiss—more a prelude to a kiss. She drew a quick breath and her eyes met his. Then, taking his hand, she led him to the bed.

He stripped quickly and slid in beside her. As he ran his hand lightly down her arm, she shivered against him.

'Are you sure about this?'

Heart pounding, Imma stared up at his beautiful face. She had never been surer about anything. Her whole body felt as though it was clamouring for him.

But as he shifted closer she felt a rush of panic. Up close and naked, there seemed to be even more of him than before. His limbs seemed more solid, and—she glanced down at his erection—he was very hard, and bigger than she'd imagined.

Her pulse accelerated. This wasn't going to work. Vicè had a wealth of sexual experience. No doubt he was expert at all kinds of lovemaking and used to sophisticated, skilful lovers. But beyond the mechanics of sex she knew absolutely nothing.

'Yes, I'm sure. Are you?'

'Am *I* sure?' He seemed to consider her question, frowning. Then, 'Yeah, of course.'

His hand moved to cover her hip, his fingers gliding over the crest of bone in a way that made her skin tingle.

'I mean, as long as you respect me in the morning...' he added.

His eyes gleamed and she started to laugh.

Dipping his head, he brushed his mouth against her. 'Tell me what you want.' His voice was warm with desire. 'What you like.'

She didn't know what she liked. She didn't know where to start. Where it would end.

'I like this...' Her finger trembled against the curve of his jaw. 'And this...' She touched his chest, the smooth contours of his muscles. 'And this.' She flattened her hand against the trail of fine dark hair that ran down the centre of his stomach.

He sucked in a breath, his pupils flaring.

'I like that too,' he said unsteadily and, lowering his mouth, he kissed her.

He kissed her lightly, then more deeply, slowing

the kiss down, slowing her pulse and her breath, kissing her so that she forgot her doubts, forgot his past— forgot everything except the touch of his mouth and the heat of his skin and the unchecked hunger in his dark eyes.

He cupped her breasts, gently thumbing each nipple, and then, taking his weight on his knees and elbows, he grazed the hardened tips with his mouth, his warm breath sending shock waves of desire up and down her body so that her stomach clenched around the ball of heat pulsing inside her.

She arched against him, pressing herself closer, wanting more of him. His fingers were sliding over her skin now, in slow, measured caresses that made a moan of pure need rise up in her throat.

Would it be like this on her wedding night? Would her husband make her feel like this? That nameless man who was yet to be chosen for her. She took a breath, fighting panic, and instantly felt him still against her.

'Cara...' He shifted his weight. 'Is this okay? Do you want me to stop?'

'No.' She splayed her hands on his chest, feeling his quickening heartbeat through her fingertips. 'I don't want you to stop. Please, don't stop.'

She couldn't admit the truth. It would be crazy to admit that she wanted this to last forever—for him to be that nameless man, to be her husband.

Reaching up, she brought his face down to hers and kissed him slowly, deepening the kiss as he pushed against her.

His hand moved across the outside of her leg, then between her thighs. Shivering, she shifted closer, lifting her hips, pressing against the hard contours of his knuckles, seeking him, wanting him to ease the ache inside her.

'Your skin is like silk,' Vicè murmured.

He pulled her closer, moulding her body against his, his mouth finding hers—and then he felt her hand enclose the heavy weight of his erection.

He cut off a groan, catching her hand in his, blood thundering in his ears.

'Not yet…not me.' Pushing her gently back on the bed, he leaned over her, kissing her deeply. 'This is all about you.'

Hooking his thumbs into her panties, he slid them down her legs. Now she was completely naked.

'Look at me,' he said softly.

Her eyes locked with his and he felt his heartbeat accelerate.

His breathing staccato, he began again at her face, tracing the outline of her lips with his tongue, kissing the curving bones of her cheeks, and then he lowered his mouth to her throat, tracking the pulse beating frenctically beneath the smooth skin, moving with deliberate, sensuous slowness down to the swell of her breasts.

Her hands slid through his hair and she pushed his head against her nipple, moaning softly as she arched her body up to meet his lips.

His heart missed a beat. He was desperately trying to centre himself. Trying to stay detached. But she was just so beautiful, so eager and responsive. He couldn't stop himself from responding to her. His need for her was like a fever in his blood.

Her nipples were taut and he sucked first one and then the other, nipping the swollen ruched tips, his erection so hard now it was almost horizontal.

Ignoring the ache in his groin, he found her mouth again, kissing her slowly, sliding his hand down over her waist and through the triangle of curls, gently probing the slick heat between her thighs.

Imma felt her head start to spin. She had never felt anything like this before. His fingers were moving inside her, his thumb brushing the nub of her clitoris, sending oscillating tremors over her skin.

Shivering, she moved against his caress, chasing the pulse beating in his hand, wanting, needing something *more* to fill the urgent hollowed-out ache inside her.

'You're killing me,' he said hoarsely.

She reached again for his groin. This time he didn't stop her, and as her fingers wrapped around his hard, swollen length, he groaned against her mouth.

'Ti voglio,' she whispered. 'I want to feel you inside me. *Ti prego.*'

Gritting his teeth, he shifted his weight and reached over to the bedside table. She heard a tearing sound. Dazed, she watched him slide a condom on.

He gazed down into her face and the dark passion in his eyes made hunger rear up inside her.

Lowering his mouth, he kissed her breasts again, licking her nipples and drawing them into his mouth, and then she felt the blunt head of his erection pushing between her thighs.

It was too big. She tensed. It would never fit inside her.

Her hands pressed against his chest, and he stopped moving, shifting his weight minutely.

'It's okay,' he murmured. 'Take your time. You just
need to get used to me.'

His voice calmed her, but it was the hunger etched
on his face that made her start to move against him.

Taking a breath, she parted her legs further. She
arched upward, straining for something she didn't understand, something just out of reach, something that
would satisfy the insistent clamouring of her body.

He moved above her and instinctively she opened
her legs wider, her breath jerking in her throat as he
rubbed the tip of his erection against the bud of her
clitoris. Curling her arms around his shoulders, wanting to feel all of him inside her, she lifted her hips and
he pushed into her.

There was a moment of sharpness and she tensed—
must have tensed, because he stilled above her. Not
wanting him to suspect her virginity—or, worse, stop—
she pulled him closer and began to move against him,
trying to regulate her breathing as her body stretched
to accommodate him.

He was fully inside her now, and his mouth found
hers as he matched himself to the rhythm of her breathing. As he started to increase his pace she felt the pulse
inside her accelerate in time to his movements.

She was panting now, lunging up towards him. Muscles she hadn't known she had were straining, pulling
apart, fraying, and she gripped his shoulders as her
whole body suddenly splintered in a rush of pleasure
so intense she could have wept.

And then he was thrusting into her, clamping her
body to his, his groans mingling with her ragged breathing as he tensed, shuddering helplessly against her.

His hands tightened in her hair and he kissed her

face, murmuring her name against the damp skin of her neck. *'Sei bellissima,'* he said softly.

She smiled, suddenly shy beneath his dark gaze. 'Was it okay for you?'

'Was it okay for me?' He laughed. 'I've never been asked that before. It was more than "okay", *cara*. It was incredible.'

'I didn't know it could be like that,' she said slowly.

How could she have imagined such dizzying pleasure was right there, at her fingertips? Her cheeks felt warm. Or rather at *his* fingertips. She had wanted it to be amazing but she had completely underestimated how it would feel, the bliss of being touched, the heat of his mouth...

His eyes roamed her face. 'What's it been like before?'

Her heart gave a jump. She could lie, but it was done now. They had made love. There was no need for secrets between them.

'It wasn't like anything.' She took a breath. 'There was no "before". You're my first—my first lover.'

Her first lover.

Vicè stared at her in silence, made mute by shock and disbelief.

She'd been a virgin.

He couldn't have been any more stunned if she'd thrown a bucket of cold water in his face.

His head was spinning. With an effort, he replayed the time they had just spent in each other's arms.

When he'd entered her—he gritted his teeth, *her actual first time*—her body had been tight, and there had been moments when she'd tensed, moments when he had felt her hesitate.

But he'd put it down to nerves over having sex with somebody new. He hadn't thought she had no experience whatsoever.

Suddenly his skin could barely contain the chaos inside his body.

He was frustrated with himself for not realising, and he felt guilty for not taking it more slowly, more gently—he would have done if he'd known. He was angry too, incomprehensibly. Angry with Ciro, for putting him in this position, but mostly with Imma.

He swallowed against the rush of questions rising in his throat.

Why hadn't she told him?

Why hadn't she said anything?

It made no sense.

But there was nothing he could do about it now. No magic spell to turn back time.

'I am?' He frowned. 'Sorry, I thought... I mean, I know you went to university, so...'

She shrugged casually, her hands trembling as she spoke. 'I didn't live in halls. My father bought me an apartment and insisted on my bodyguards going everywhere with me.'

'So those "others" you mentioned...you didn't...?'

Imma shook her head. 'I never wanted any of them in that way. Not like I wanted you.' She hesitated. 'Is it a problem?'

She was staring up at him, and the expression on her face made him swear silently. He needed to make this all right, and fast, or risk blowing everything.

Shaking his head, he touched her cheek. 'Quite the

contrary.' His face twisted. 'I can't believe I'm saying this, but I like it that I'm your first.'

Imma stared at him, her pulse beating out of time.

'Actually, I'm a little embarrassed by how happy it makes me feel,' he added.

Her stomach clenched and blood rushed into her pelvis. Her body was rippling back to life as he pulled her closer.

Breathing out unsteadily, he buried his face in her neck. 'Imma, do you think it's possible for two people to fall in love in a single day?'

Her heart lurched against her ribs. His dark eyes were soft and steady on her face, but she could hear the shake in his voice.

She took a deep breath. 'I do,' she said softly.

'And could you maybe see yourself saying *I do*?' He stared down at her. 'If I asked you to marry me.'

'You don't have to marry me,' she said shakily. 'It was my decision not to say anything. I should have told you I was a virgin—'

'That's not why I want to marry you.'

His arms tightened around her, and she knew he was telling the truth.

'I know it sounds crazy, but I have to marry you—there's no other option for me.'

The poetry of his words made her heart swell.

She was too choked to speak, but as he lowered his mouth to hers she leaned into him, her hands threading through his hair, and kissed him fiercely.

They made love again, and afterwards she fell asleep in his arms.

She was still wrapped in his arms sometime later,

when she woke in the early hours, and for a moment she lay on her side, watching Vicè sleep.

There were no words to describe how she was feeling. She was happy—had never been happier—but 'happy' felt too ordinary, too small a word to describe what had just happened.

It was everything she'd wanted for her first time. He had wanted her for herself, just as she had wanted him, and his desire had made her feel sensual. Confident. Powerful. Even when her body had dissolved into hot, endless need.

She still felt as if she was glowing inside.

And it wasn't just the sex.

It was Vicè.

She had fallen helplessly in love with him. And, incredibly, he felt the same way about her. He must do to have proposed.

Her heart trembled

She might not have his experience, but she had learned enough about the world to know that a man like Vicè didn't propose marriage after every sexual encounter.

Given his track record with women, he must have been hoping simply to seduce her. It had probably never crossed his mind that he would fall in love any more than it had hers.

Glancing over at him, she felt her throat tighten.

He was so beautiful, so gorgeously masculine, all muscle and smooth golden skin, and he'd been so generous. Remembering how his body had felt, on hers and in hers, her muscles tensed.

Suddenly she was hot and damp and aching.

It had been so good.

Felt so right.

His weight and the press of his mouth…the rush of his heartbeat.

Could she wake him?

She bit her lip. Would that be greedy? Too forward?

He shifted in his sleep, turning his face into the crook of his arm, and she breathed out unevenly.

She was so, *so* happy. The only thing that would make it even more perfect was if she could share her happiness with Claudia. But it was too early—and anyway it was her sister's wedding night.

She frowned. Across the room, she could hear her phone ringing. Slipping out of bed, she picked it up, her heart fluttering with joy. It was Claudia. But of course it was—they had always had the ability to communicate almost telepathically.

She tiptoed out of the bedroom, closing the door softly behind her. 'Hey, you! I was just—'

'Oh, Immie, something terrible has happened.' Claudia's voice was high and trembling.

Imma's breath scrabbled inside her chest. 'Don't cry, *mia cara*. What is it? Tell me.'

'It's all a lie, Immie. He doesn't love me.'

Her heart pounded fiercely. 'Of course he does—'

'He doesn't. He didn't know I was there and I heard him talking on the phone—'

'That can't be right…' The phone felt slippery in Imma's hand and she clutched it more tightly. 'Ciro loves you.'

'No, he doesn't, Immie. He doesn't. He just married me to get revenge on Papà. And Vicenzu is planning to do the same to you.'

The room swayed. For a moment she couldn't breathe. Her lungs felt as though they were full of sand.

It couldn't be true. Claudia must have made a mistake. Vicè wouldn't do that—

But as her sister began to cry she knew that he had.

CHAPTER FOUR

ROLLING OVER ONTO his side, Vicè shifted against the pillow, his hand reaching across the bed for—

His eyes snapped open.

For Imma.

But the bed was empty.

He raised himself up on his elbow, his pulse accelerating as he heard the sound of running water from the bathroom. He glanced at the clock by the bed, realising how late in the day it was. She must be showering.

Only it wasn't the thought of a naked Imma with water streaming over the soft curves of her body that was making his pulse beat faster. It was the sharp, shocking realisation that he had been reaching out for her—for the daughter of his enemy.

Except she hadn't felt like his enemy—not when she'd been moving on top of him with her hair tumbling over her shoulders and a dazed look in those incredible olive green eyes.

When she'd walked out of the bathroom last night, naked except for that tiny wisp of underwear, he'd forgotten all those weeks of anger and doubt. In that moment he had simply been a man swept away by lust.

He gritted his teeth. But now his feelings were less

simple—they were downright confused, in fact, and for one very obvious reason.

He hadn't signed up for taking her virginity.

In fact, he'd never slept with a virgin before, and if he'd been going to start it wouldn't have been with *this* woman.

Taking Imma's virginity felt like a bond—a connection between them that didn't fit well with the task in hand. And yet...

He might have made a joke of it earlier, but almost against his will—flying in the face of everything he knew to be logical—he liked being her first lover.

His skin felt suddenly hot and taut. Even to admit that privately to himself blew his mind. When had he turned into such a caveman?

But there was no point in pretending. Satisfaction that he had been her first still resonated inside him.

And affected him on the outside too, apparently.

Gritting his teeth, he lifted the sheet away from his erection. He didn't understand what was happening to him. Imma was very beautiful, and she felt even better than she looked. But he was remembering how she'd fallen asleep, with her body curled around his. He let go of a breath he hadn't realised he was holding.

No matter how attractive the woman, or how intense his desire, he had never felt even the slightest impulse to hold any of his lovers in his arms while he slept.

It must have been finding out she was a virgin. There was no other explanation.

Rolling onto his back, he frowned up at the ceiling. He was irritated at having to feel anything but his usual sense of repletion. He certainly hadn't planned on dealing with all this complicated stuff.

But was it really that complicated? So she'd been a virgin? So what?

She was an adult, and she had wanted sex as much as he had. Getting fixated on being her first lover was making him lose sight of what mattered—the fact that for once he'd done what he'd set out to do.

It had been a playbook seduction. He'd used his hands, his mouth, his body expertly to turn her on, touching her and tormenting her until she had melted into him, her moans of ecstasy filling the silent room.

Agreed, her virginity had added a layer of confusion—but surely it would make the likelihood of her marrying him and therefore getting back the business a shoo-in.

He was going to push for the soonest date possible for their wedding. After that, all that would remain would be for him to persuade her to sign the paperwork.

Then it would be done.

Revenge would be theirs.

But he was jumping ahead of himself. His moment of triumph would need to be savoured properly with Ciro, over a cigar, and probably some of that bourbon his brother loved so much. Right now there were other things to savour.

His pulse twitched and he felt hunger course through his veins like a caffeine rush.

So why not simply enjoy the ride?

He glanced over at the bathroom door. Maybe he would join her in that shower, after all…

But just as he was about to throw back the sheet, the door to the bathroom opened. Remembering her entrance last night, he felt his gaze narrow—but this time Imma wasn't naked. In fact—disappointingly—she was fully clothed.

His eyes drifted lazily over the simple white cotton dress she was wearing and he felt a pulse of heat bumping over his skin. He wasn't averse to watching her take it off.

Sprawling back against the pillows, he lifted his eyes to hers and smiled. 'Hi.'

'Hi,' she said quietly.

She didn't move, just stood in the doorway.

'Did you sleep well?'

She nodded. 'Yes, thank you.'

'Are you okay? I mean—'

She nodded again. 'Everything's fine.'

He felt relief slide over his skin. He'd been a little worried that, having had time to think, she might want to do some kind of post-mortem. Clearly, though, she had other things on her mind.

She took a deep breath. 'Vicè, last night you asked me to marry you. I wondered if you meant it? Or if you just got carried away in the heat of the moment?'

'Of course I meant it.' Throwing back the sheet, he got up and walked swiftly around the bed to where she stood in the doorway. 'I want to marry you. I want to do it as soon as possible. Only...'

He hesitated, a rush of triumph sweeping over his skin as her eyes searched his face. *He had done it*. She was hooked. His father's business was as good as his.

'Only what?'

'Only I don't remember you actually saying yes.'

'Oh!' she gasped in a rush. 'Then, yes... I will marry you. But first there's something I want to do.'

There was only a sliver of space between them. Her gaze dropped to his naked body and he felt his groin harden again in time with his accelerating heartbeat. *Really? She was going to...?*

She slapped him across the face.

He swore. 'What the hell—'

'You are a *monster*.'

The softness in her voice was gone, and it was gone from her eyes too. She looked and sounded coldly furious.

'You and that despicable brother of yours.'

She slapped his other cheek, equally hard.

'How could he do that to her? How could you both be so cruel?'

Stunned, his face stinging, he caught her hand as she lifted it to strike him again. A flush of panic and confusion swirled in his chest.

'I don't know what—'

She struggled against his grip. '*Basta!* Enough!' She tugged her hand free. 'I've had enough of your lies. I know none of this is real, Vicenzu. I know because I've read the texts you sent your brother. And I've heard his voicemail.'

She pulled his phone from her pocket and he stared at it in silence. A cold, dull ache was spreading over his skin, turning his blood to ice.

'You didn't bother locking it—but then I suppose you didn't think you needed to. I mean, why would you be worried about *me*? A woman who was stupid enough to gift-wrap her virginity for you.'

'That's not fair!' he snarled. 'If you'd told me, I would have—'

'You would have what?' She folded her arms across her chest, her green eyes wide with contempt. 'Given up? Gone home? *Yeah, right,*' she jeered. 'And forgotten all about taking back your precious olive oil company. I think not. You might be careless about most things—like the truth…' She paused, her expression not just hardening, but ossifying. 'But clearly you care about that.'

He flinched inwardly, the truth of her words slicing through him to the bone.

But this conversation was always going to happen, he told himself quickly. It wasn't as if he and Imma had ever been going to celebrate their ruby wedding in forty years, like his parents had.

The memory of the last time he'd visited his parents' home made his spine tense painfully. At the time he'd vaguely registered that his father looked a little tired and seemed a little quieter than usual, but it had been easy—shamefully easy—to just tell himself that his dad was getting old.

Except now Alessandro would never get old. That was on him, even more than on his brother, but the person really responsible for this mess was this woman's father: Cesare Buscetta.

She held up his phone. 'Perhaps you've forgotten what you wrote? Perhaps you'd like me to read your text to you? Just to remind you.'

'I know what I wrote, Imma,' he said coldly. He met her gaze and then, reaching down, picked up his clothes from last night, pulling them on with deliberate unconcern.

Her eyes were sharp, like shards of broken glass. 'You know what makes all this so much worse? I already *knew* about your reputation with women. I *knew* you couldn't be trusted. But then we talked, and you made me believe that people had been wrong about you.

That you weren't some spoilt playboy with nothing in his head except living *la dolce vita*.'

She shook her head, and even though he was angry he couldn't stop his brain from focusing on the way her still damp hair was turning her white dress transparent.

'And I was right.' She stared at him, contempt mingling with loathing in her green eyes. 'You're not just a spoilt playboy—you're also a vicious, unprincipled liar.'

'Says the woman who didn't bother telling me she was a virgin,' he snarled, feeling the dam inside him breaking.

A part of him knew that he was only angry with her because he was in the wrong. He had seduced her. Methodically, cold-bloodedly pursuing her at the wedding, gaining her trust, then using all his charm to woo her into bed.

And all the while he'd told himself that she deserved it. He'd thought he had her all figured out. Thought she was a silent witness to her father's behaviour.

Only then she'd told him she was a virgin, and for some reason that had changed everything. It had made him feel responsible, guilty, and that wasn't fair.

'You should have told me,' he said.

'About my virginity?' Her eyes narrowed. 'Why? What difference would it have made?'

He was in a blind fury now. 'It would have made a difference to me!'

She was either incredibly naive or disingenuous if she thought that any man wouldn't want to know whether a woman had ever had sex before.

'Oh, and this is all about you. You and your stupid vendetta.' Her lip curled. 'You were lying to me, Vicè. And you would still be lying to me now if I hadn't confronted you. Tossing a few rose petals on the bed and lighting some candles wouldn't have changed anything.'

Porca miseria! Vicè stared at her, hearing her words pinballing around inside his brain. He wasn't talking about rose petals and candles. He was talking about the rules of interaction between couples.

'So what if I lied?' he asked. 'You lie all the time. To me. To other people. To yourself—'

'Excuse me?' Her voice was a whisper of loathing.

'All that garbage about your father wishing he could have "helped" mine sooner.' *Helped!* The word curdled in his mouth. 'Turning a blind eye to his arm-twisting doesn't absolve you. It was your monstrous father hounding him, breaking him down month after month, that sent my father to an early grave—as you very well know.'

'That's not true.' She spat the words at him. 'Papà told me what happened. How your father had over-stretched himself. How he came and asked to be bought out. Maybe he didn't want you and Ciro to know the truth.' She gave him a withering glance. 'I mean, why would he? He clearly knew neither of his sons had what was needed to save his life's work.'

Vicè flinched inwardly. One son certainly hadn't.

A stiletto of pain stabbed him beneath the ribs. Pain followed by rage. With her, for seeing what he was so desperate to hide, and with himself for not having been the son his father had needed.

Instead he had been an additional burden in Alessandro's time of need. For in trying to protect him, his son, his father had been left with nobody to turn to.

'Your father is a thief and a thug,' he said slowly. 'He stole the business my great-grandfather founded and the house where my parents lived their whole married life. Thanks to him, my mother lost her husband and her home all in one day.'

Her face turned pale, but then she rallied, lifting her chin so that her gaze was level with his. 'And is your mother in on this too?'

The tightness in his chest was unbearable. '*What? No.* My mother is a saint. She's the sweetest person on earth.'

'I thought so.'

Her eyes hadn't left his face, and now there was something unsettling in her steady, stinging gaze.

'That's why we're going to get married,' she said.

He stared at her in confusion. *Get married? She still wanted to marry him?* Surely she was joking?

As though she could read his mind, she gave a humourless laugh. 'What's the matter, Vicè? Have you had a change of heart?' Her eyes narrowed. 'Oh, sorry, I forgot—you don't have a heart.'

Imma swallowed past the lump in her throat. It hurt to breathe. It hurt to speak. It hurt to look into his eyes and see nothing but hatred and hostility where only hours earlier she had thought she'd seen love.

She was such a fool. Had she really believed that this beautiful angry man could see past her defensiveness and gauche manner to what was inside? To value and desire what he saw there?

Their night together had been perfect, unrepeatable, miraculous—so that even when he had pulled her closer, or she had reached out for him, it had felt illusory…like an all too vivid dream.

And now she was living in a nightmare of her own

making, and no amount of daylight was ever going to wake her up.

If only she could go back in time—back to before Claudia had called her, back to that moment when she had been held in the muscular warmth of his arms. When her heart, her pride, had still been intact.

But it was too late for regrets. All that mattered now was making him pay. And she was going to keep telling herself that until it felt true.

His face darkened. 'And you, like the rest of your rotten, corrupted family, have no soul.'

Her eyes blazed into his. 'You are nothing to me now—just as I was nothing to you.'

She'd felt something—something real—but for him it had all been a trick, a con, a hoax.

The pain made her want to throw up.

He took a step forward. 'Great reason to get married.'

'It's about on a par with yours.' Pushing past the pain, she filled her voice with contempt. 'You slept with me under false pretences, Vicè. You faked your way into my bed. At least now we both know what's real and what isn't.'

He shook his head. 'What happened last night in your bed *was* real. You wanted me as much as I wanted you.'

Oh, he was good. He was so convincing—so plausible. Even now, when they both knew the truth, he made it sound as if he really believed what he was saying.

She shook her head. 'Actually, you *wanted* my father's business.'

Breathing out raggedly, she watched his face darken.

'No, I wanted *my* father's business.'

'Then you should have approached me with an offer.'

'I'm not going to pay for what was stolen from me.'

The hardness in his voice pressed against the bruise on her heart. The pain of trying to pretend spread out inside her like a rain cloud. Tears pricked behind her eyes and she blinked them away furiously, determined not to show any weakness in front of him.

'No, *I* paid. With my virginity.'

She felt a rush of shame and misery, remembering how her body had softened and melted from the heat of him.

His flinch was small, fleeting, but she saw it.

'Is that the going price for an olive oil company these days?' she taunted.

A flush of colour crept over his cheeks, but his eyes were cold. When he spoke his voice was colder still. 'For the last time, I didn't know you were a virgin.'

'Don't try and pretend you have a conscience, Vicenzu.' Her simmering pain gave way to an even hotter anger. 'You wanted to marry me and you will. Only it will be on my terms. Not yours. And if you refuse then I will find your mother and tell her exactly how you and your brother have behaved,' she said, her voice shaking slightly. 'I will tell her what kind of men the boys she raised have become.'

Her threat was empty. She wouldn't do it. She didn't want to marry him, and nor would she do anything to hurt Audenzia.

But she wanted to hurt him like he'd hurt her, and this was the only way she could think to do it.

His face hardened and the look in his eyes made her want to weep.

'I thought your father was a monster, but you...you are something else.'

And she had thought Vicenzu was the kind of man

who crossed any number of boundaries, but not ruthlessly or with wanton cruelty.

Jabbing his phone into his chest, she met his gaze head-on. 'Yes, I am. I'm your nemesis, Vicenzu.'

Her face was aching with the effort of blanking out the beauty of his high cheekbones and full mouth… the mouth that had so recently kissed her into a state of feverish rapture.

His eyes narrowed. 'You really are Daddy's little girl, aren't you? Except that he uses threats and then violence to get what he wants.'

Smiling bitterly, she shook her head. 'What happened to *"what they can't find out, they make up"*?'

He stared at her incredulously. 'I wasn't talking about your father.'

'Well, you couldn't have been talking about yourself. Nobody in their right mind could make this up.' Her voice rose. 'How could you do this to me? How could you be so cruel?'

'You think *I'm* cruel?' He took a rough breath, his face hardening. 'Me? No, I'm just an amateur, *cara*.' He typed something into his phone, scrolled down the screen. 'This is the real deal. Here—' Letting his contempt show, he pressed the phone into her hand. 'You like reading my messages? Read these and then tell me who the bad guy is.'

She stared at him. Her lungs felt as if they were on fire. 'I don't need to. *You* are the bad guy, Vicenzu.'

And, sidestepping past him, she walked quickly away—going nowhere, just wanting, needing, to get as far away as possible from his cold-eyed distaste and the wreckage of her romantic dreams.

She half expected him to come after her, as he had

last night. But of course last night he'd been playing her. Last night he'd only come after her because he'd been playing his part, doing whatever it took to get the family business back.

Whatever it took.

Like having sex with her.

The thought that having sex with her had been one step en route to the bigger prize, a means to trap and manipulate her, made her feel sick.

She had wanted her first time to be perfect. To be her choice and not just an expected consequence of her marriage vows. Had wanted it to be with Vicè, because in her naivety—idiot that she'd been—she had liked and trusted him.

And when he'd walked towards her at the wedding, his dancing eyes and teasing laughter trailing promises of happiness, she'd fallen in love with him.

As she reached the terrace tears began to fill her eyes and she brushed them away angrily.

She had been stubborn and vain. Ignoring and defying her father's words of warning and letting herself be flattered by Vicè's lies. Her pain was deserved. But Claudia's...

Her eyes filled with tears again, and this time she let them roll down her cheeks. She had let her sister down. Worse, she had broken her word.

She had been eight years old when she made that promise—too young to understand that her mother was dying, but old enough to understand the promise she was making. A promise to take care of her younger sister, to protect her and keep her safe in the kind of cruel, unjust world that would leave two young children motherless.

She had always kept her word. Protecting Claudia at school, and at home too. Shielding her from the full force of Cesare's outbursts and trying to boost her confidence by encouraging her love of cooking and gardening.

Only now she had broken that promise.

Remembering her sister's stunned, tearful call, she felt another stab of guilt. Claudia was her priority. She would do whatever her sister wanted—help in any way she needed. Then she would face her father.

But first…

Her fingers tightened around the phone in her hand—Vicè's phone.

She found what she was looking for easily—an email from the family lawyer, Vito Neglia, to Ciro and Vicenzu, plus further emails between Alessandro and Neglia.

She scrolled down the screen, her eyes following the lines of text.

It made difficult reading.

Alessandro Trapani had been unlucky—machinery had broken and mistakes had been made. He had taken out a loan with the bank and then his troubles had begun to escalate. There had been accidents at work, then more problems with machinery, and he had started to struggle to meet the repayments.

Her heart jolted as her father's name leapt out from the screen. But she had been right, she thought with a rush of relief. Cesare had offered cash for the business with the proviso that the sale would include the family estate. She took a steadying breath. It was just as her father had told her. Papà had only been trying to help.

She glanced back down at the screen and some of her relief began to ooze away.

Alessandro had refused her father's offer. But then he hadn't been able to pay one of his suppliers—and, with the bank putting increasing pressure on him over the repayments, he'd gone back to Cesare.

This time her father had offered twenty percent less.

With no other options left, Alessandro had had no choice but to accept.

But that was just *business*, she told herself, trying to push back against the leaden feeling in her stomach. Probably if the circumstances had been reversed Alessandro would have done exactly the same.

Clearly Neglia didn't agree with her.

He had done some digging around and, although he had found no direct link to her father, there was clearly no doubt in the lawyer's mind that Trapani employees had been bribed to sabotage the machinery.

And her father had been behind it.

Imma's throat worked as she struggled to swallow her shock. She felt sick on the inside. Her skin was cold and clammy and her head was spinning.

She didn't want it to be true.

But the facts were stark and unforgiving.

Cesare had used bribery and intimidation to ruin a man's business and steal it away from him. The fact that he had also demanded Alessandro's home made her heart break into pieces.

Hot tears stung the back of her eyes. No wonder Ciro and Vicè hated him. But, whatever her father had done, it didn't give them the right to punish her and Claudia, and she hated both of them for that.

Only despite everything she had read, she couldn't

bring herself to hate her father. It wasn't an excuse, but she knew he would have done it for her and for Claudia.

Cesare was not stupid. He'd heard the rumours about his 'friends' and his shady dealings. And she knew that he wanted something different for his daughters. That was why they had been educated at the convent. That was why they'd been raised like princesses in a tower.

And that was why he had used every trick in the book to acquire a 'clean' business and a beautiful family estate—as gifts for his beloved girls.

The world suddenly felt very fragile.

She forced air into her lungs, tried to focus.

She couldn't hate her father, but she couldn't face moving back home either. She needed space, and time to think about all of this—about her part in it and her future.

Her future.

She sank down in one of the chairs, wrapping her arms around her stomach. She felt incredibly, brutally tired. Tired of not knowing who she was or what she wanted.

Her heart pounded. She had thought she wanted Vicè—that he had wanted her. She had been wrong about that too. And yet on one level she didn't regret what had happened. Having sex with him had unlocked a part of herself she hadn't known existed.

She had discovered a woman who was wild and alive and demanding, and she liked that woman. She wanted to find out more about her, and that was another reason she needed time and space.

Time and space—those words again.

She wouldn't have either living at home with Papà. But sooner or later she was going to have to tell him that she had slept with Vicè, and then he would insist on her marrying someone of his choosing.

Her pulse slowed and she sat up straight, biting her lip, listening to the distant sound of the waves.

Maybe, though, there was another option...

Clenching his jaw, Vicè stared around the empty bedroom.

He was still in shock. The script he'd planned for today had unravelled so fast, so dramatically, and in a way he could hardly believe possible.

Just when everything had been falling into place so beautifully.

Everything.

She'd even agreed to marry him.

So how come he was standing here with his face still stinging and her ultimatum ringing in his ears?

Behind him the tangled bed sheets were like a rebuke or a taunt and, feeling as if the walls were starting to shrink around him, he crossed the room, yanking open the door and stepping through it in time with his pounding heartbeat.

It was his fault.

Actually, no, it was hers.

If she had told him the truth about being a virgin in the first place he might not have been so distracted, so caught off balance.

He might even have locked his phone.

His chest tightened. How could he have been so unforgivably stupid and careless? When Ciro found out he was going to go ballistic. He might never speak to him again.

The one consolation in this whole mess was that

Ciro had already managed to get the house back. He knew his brother: Ciro was a fast worker. Claudia had agreed to sign over the house before she'd learned the truth, and those documents would be signed and witnessed by now.

But what did he have to show for himself?

Niente, that was what!

He had nothing.

He gave a humourless smile. He was trapped on an island with a woman who basically wanted to cut off his *palle* and fry them up for brunch.

Glancing back into the bedroom, he ran a hand over his face, wishing he could as easily smooth over the last few hours of his life.

The shock of being unmasked had shaken him more than he cared to admit—as had Imma's threat to speak to his mother. Although now he'd had a chance to cool off he knew she'd been bluffing.

But what had really got under his skin was the sudden devastating loss of the woman who had melted into him just hours earlier.

Gone was the passion, the inhibition of the night, when she had arched against him, her body moving like a flame in the darkness. Now in her eyes he might as well be something that had crawled out from under a particularly dank and slimy rock.

And, even though he knew logically that it shouldn't matter what Imma thought about him, he didn't like how it made him feel. Didn't like being made to feel like he was the bad guy.

There was only one bad guy and that was her father.

From somewhere nearby a phone buzzed twice. Glancing down, he saw that it was his.

It was sitting on a small table and he felt his stomach tense. Imma must have left it for him. Feeling a sharp stab of guilt and misery, he picked it up, swearing under his breath.

His stomach dipped. It was Ciro.

His brother's message was short and to the point.

I can't talk now, but it's all gone belly-up here so you need to pull your finger out.

For a moment he let his finger hover over his brother's number, and then, swearing loudly this time, he pocketed the phone.

He couldn't deal with his brother right now. He had to get his head straight first.

He was clenching his jaw so tightly that it ached.

Nine weeks ago he would have walked away.

But nine weeks ago he still had a father.

Tilting his head back, he closed his eyes. He still couldn't believe that he would never see Alessandro again. His father had been his mentor, his defender—more than that, he had been his hero. He had been the best of men...fair, kind, generous and loving.

Opening his eyes, he breathed out unevenly. He'd given up any hope of ever being his father's equal a long time ago, but he could do this one thing and do it right.

He had let down Papà in life; he would not do so now.

Imma was not going to have everything her own way.

He'd sat around listening to his father and Ciro talk business enough to know that she had overplayed her hand with him, and let her emotions get the better of her. In her anger, she had threatened the very thing he had wanted all along.

He *would* be her husband—but he was not going to walk away empty-handed. He was going to take back the Trapani Olive Oil Company and there would be nothing his future 'wife' could do about it.

He found her out by the pool, staring down at the smooth turquoise surface of the water. In her white dress, and with her long dark hair flowing over her shoulders, she looked as young and untested as her name suggested, and her slender body reminded him of the delicate honey-scented sweet peas that were his mother's favourite flowers.

It was hard to believe she was the same woman who had threatened to tell Audenzia the truth about everything he and Ciro had been doing. He gritted his teeth. Hard, but not impossible.

She turned towards him, folding her arms high across her ribs. But even without the defensive gesture he would have known that she had looked at the emails on his phone.

Her eyes were slightly swollen and she looked pale, more delicate. He felt a pang of guilt, but pushed it away. The truth hurt—so what? His mother had been widowed and forced to leave her home. That was real suffering.

'I read the emails,' she said quietly. 'I don't know what to say except that I'm sorry for how my father acted, and for what I said earlier about talking to your mother.' She took a breath. 'I was angry, and upset, but I want you to know that I would never do anything to hurt her. I know she had nothing to do with this.' Her eyes met his, steady, accusatory. 'I would never punish an innocent bystander.'

Her words stung. No doubt she'd intended they

should. But he was surprised by her apology. He hadn't expected that—not from anyone bearing the Buscetta surname. Only if she thought that was somehow going to be enough...

He took a step towards her. 'And the marriage proposal?' he said softly.

Her green eyes narrowed. 'Yours or mine?' she shot back.

'Does it matter?'

'I suppose not.'

He heard the catch in her voice, and before he could stop himself he said, 'So tell me, Imma, if you're not looking for revenge then why exactly do you want to marry me?'

Her arms clenched and, watching the fabric of her dress tighten over her nipples, he felt his pulse snake, remembering how just hours earlier they had hardened against his tongue.

She shrugged. 'My father is a traditional Sicilian male. Very traditional. Now that you and I have had sex he'll expect us to marry, and if we don't he'll find another husband for me.' Lifting her chin, she twisted her mouth into a small, tight smile. 'Essentially you're the lesser of two evils, Vicè.'

Chewing her words over inside his head, he felt his gut tense. *Wow!* That was a backhander. It certainly wasn't something he'd ever been called before.

She took a quick breath. 'If we marry, then obviously I'll be your wife legally. But in reality you'll just be there. In the background.'

In the background.

He wasn't sure if it was her disparaging description

of his upcoming role or her haughty manner, but he felt a pulse of anger beat across his skin.

'Sounds relaxing. Will I need to get dressed?'

That got to her. She wanted him still. He could see it in the flush of her cheeks and the restless pulse in her throat. Watching her pupils flare, he felt his own anger shift into desire.

Ignoring his question, she said coolly, 'Before we go any further, you should know that I have a condition.'

A condition?

'Is that so?' Taking a step towards her, he held her gaze.

She nodded. 'The marriage will last a year. That's long enough for it to look real. If we manage our diaries, then we shouldn't have to intrude into one another's lives beyond what's necessary.'

He stared at her in silence. All his life women had fawned over him, flattered and chased him. But now Imma was basically treating him like a footstool.

'I have a condition too,' he said silkily.

Seeing her swallow, he felt a flicker of satisfaction.

'I will stay married to you for a year. But I want it in writing now that you will sign the Trapani Olive Oil Company over to me at the end of that year.'

She searched his face. Probably she thought he was joking. When she realised he was being serious, she started shaking her head. 'You can't expect me to—' she began.

He cut her off. 'Oh, but I do. I find managing my diary very dull, so I'll need *some* incentive.'

He enjoyed the flash of outrage in her eyes almost as much as the way she bit down on her lip—presumably to stop herself from saying something she'd regret.

'Is that going to be a problem? Maybe you'd rather go back to bed and thrash all this out there instead.'

Silence followed his deliberately provocative remark, and he waited to see how she would respond, his body tensing painfully in anticipation of her accepting his challenge.

Two spots of colour flared on her cheeks and he saw her hands curl into fists. She wanted to thump him. Or kiss him. Or maybe both.

And, actually, either would be preferable to this tight-lipped disdain.

But after a moment she said stiffly, 'No, I would not.'

'Shame,' he drawled. 'Still, there's always the wedding night to look forward to.'

'Yes, there is.' She lifted her chin. 'But we'll be enjoying it in separate rooms. Just to be clear, this marriage is purely for show, Vicè. You won't be sharing my bed. Or having sex with me.'

Vicè felt his smile harden.

He'd already had to be celibate in the run-up to his brother's wedding. Not out of choice, but Ciro had insisted, and in the end he'd grudgingly accepted that any hint of scandal would ruin his chances of seducing Imma before he had even got to meet her.

Those nine weeks had left his body aching with sexual frustration. And now she was suggesting that that sentence should be extended to a year.

'Obviously you won't be having sex with anyone else either,' she added coldly. 'I won't have my family's name dragged through the mud by your libido.'

Their eyes met. 'I wouldn't worry about that, *cara*. Your father wallows in something far nastier than mud.'

His words drained the colour from her cheeks, but he

told himself that a woman who was prepared to enter willingly into this kind of marriage deserved no compassion on his part.

'That's rich, coming from you,' she said shakily. 'The man who seduced a virgin for revenge.'

He felt his gut twist. But he wasn't going to feel guilty about that. She should have told him—given him a choice about whether to do things differently.

She lifted one slender wrist and gazed down at her expensive gold watch. 'If you're done insulting me, then a simple yes or no will suffice.'

No. Absolutely not. Never. Not if my life depended on it.

He thought about his life before…*la dolce vita.*

A life of leisure and pleasure. A sweet life.

And then he thought about his mother, and his father, and the promise he had made to his brother.

'Yes,' he said.

CHAPTER FIVE

So she really was going to go through with this.

Glancing out of the window of the taxi, Imma felt her fingers tighten around the small posy of lilies of the valley in her lap. Beside her, his dark eyes shielded behind even darker glasses, his fingers pointedly entwined with hers, Vicè sat in silence.

To anyone else he would seem the perfect groom. Young, handsome, intent on marrying the woman he loved.

She swallowed past the ache in her throat. But of course he was good at pretending.

They had left the island and returned to the mainland, 'borrowed' Cesare's private jet and flown to Gibraltar. They had arrived in late last night, and booked into a discreet hotel on the edge of town, near the Botanic Gardens.

Separate rooms, obviously.

Not that it was really necessary. He might be almost painfully attentive in public, but as soon as they were alone he barely lifted his eyes to meet hers, choosing instead to stare at his phone.

And it hurt. Hurt in a way that seemed utterly illogical.

Or just stupid.

Yes, 'stupid' was the only way to describe this hollowed-out feeling of loss for something that had been so fleeting and false.

It didn't help that all the preparations had been so rushed and furtive, but she couldn't risk Cesare finding out and intervening.

Thinking about her father made her chest ache. She loved him still, but right now she didn't trust him—and she didn't trust herself to be around him. She was too angry and confused about everything she had found out, and her desolation and the sense of betrayal were still too raw.

She had no idea what to say or do next. But she did know that she didn't want anything to do with what he'd done to Alessandro. Which was why she'd agreed to hand over the business to Vicè in a year's time.

If she hadn't needed a bargaining chip to get some space and time away from her father she would have handed it over today. She hated owning the thing he wanted—hated knowing that it was the only reason he was here, sitting beside her in the car, on their way to a register office.

Her chest tightened. If they had been other people, or if the circumstances had been different, then maybe all this haste and secrecy would be exciting, impulsive and romantic. But instead it just felt sneaky.

Even though she had texted her father to say that she was at the villa, she kept expecting him to call, demanding to know when she was coming home. Obviously she hadn't told him she was in Gibraltar, and that made her nervous too.

But, judging by the long, rambling and gleeful voicemail Cesare had just left her, she had been worrying for no reason.

He hadn't been fretting over her absence at all; instead he had been shooting boar on the Di Gualtieri estate.

A shiver scuttled down her spine. Stefano di Gualtieri was a fabulously wealthy local landowner and the great-grandson of Sicilian nobility. He was her father's age, and in her opinion he was a bore of a different kind—and a snob. But, despite her hinting as much, she knew Cesare saw him as a possible suitor for her hand in marriage.

Imma exhaled softly, trying to still the jittery feeling in her chest. If her father knew what she was about to do…

But his prospective anger was not the only reason she wanted to keep off his radar for as long as possible. Since reading those emails, her world—everything she had taken for granted about the man who had raised her—had begun to look as fragile as the tiny, delicate bell-shaped flowers in her hand.

She'd thought she knew her father so well. His moods, his brusqueness, his maddening and stifling overprotectiveness. Now, though, she felt as if she didn't know him at all.

Obviously she'd heard the rumours about him, but her father had always brushed them off: yes, some of his friends were a little rough. You had to be tough where he'd grown up—that was just how it was. And he wasn't going to turn his back on his mates. What kind of friend would do that?

'That's why people say these things about me. They're jealous, piccioncina mia. *They hate me for*

dragging myself up out of the gutter so they scrape over my past...invent stories.'

It reminded her of what Vicè had said about people making up what they didn't know, and the thought that he had this, of all things, in common with her father made her want to leap out of the car while it was still moving.

Finding out that Cesare had behaved so ruthlessly made her feel sick. But finding out that he'd lied to her had been the reason why she'd finally decided to marry Vicè.

Okay, maybe at first she'd wanted revenge. Part of her still did. And she hadn't been lying when she'd told Vicè that he was the lesser of two evils. Her father would find her a husband, and she shuddered to think who he might choose.

But all her life she had struggled to know herself, and this revelation about her father made her feel she knew herself even less. Marriage to Vicè would at least give her the freedom to think about what she wanted to happen next.

And so this morning they had met with a notary, to complete the necessary paperwork. And now they were on their way to the register office.

Shifting in her seat, she glanced down at her dark blue polka-dot dress. It was the same one she'd worn to Claudia's wedding. And she hated it.

Not because it was a little boring, and cut for an older, more mature woman. But because it was so tied up with the now crushed romantic dreams of her little sister, and those few hours when Imma had mistakenly, humiliatingly, believed that Vicè was interested in her.

She could have bought another dress, but that would

have defeated the object. She needed this reminder of where vanity and self-delusion led. And anyway she wouldn't have known what to buy. What was the correct dress code for a marriage of convenience?

Her stomach clenched—doubt gripping her again. She could stop this now. Tell the driver to pull over... tell Vicenzu to get out.

Only then what?

Go back to the life she'd had?

Pretend that none of this had happened or mattered?

Blanking her mind, she sat up straighter. She didn't know if she could go back to her old life. And where could she go, what could she do, if she didn't return to it?

She didn't know that either. And that was why she would go through with this ceremony.

That way, at least she would have time to find the answers to all the questions swirling inside her head.

Feeling Imma shift beside him, Vicè felt his body tense. She was a good actress. Not for one moment would anyone guess that she was marrying him out of spite.

The solid rectangular shape of his phone pressing against his ribs reminded him of the brief but reassuring message his brother had sent.

Have secured the house. Keep your promise.

He should be pleased—and he was. And yet it would be such a relief if, just for once, his brother messed up. But of course—Ciro being Ciro—he had turned everything around. So now it was just him hurtling towards a broken bridge on a runaway train.

In the street, a group of young men jostled against the car, shoving each other and laughing at some shared joke. They looked so happy. And free.

He bit down on a sudden rush of envy. A week ago that would have been him. Now he was marrying a woman he hated. And she hated him.

But it would be worth it. For in a year the Trapani Olive Oil Company would belong to his family again.

'We're here.'

She turned to face him and smiled, and even though he knew it was for show his breath stuck in his throat. She shouldn't be marrying him like this. Where was her father now? Her bodyguards? Didn't anyone care that she was doing this?

He thought back to the way her face had changed when he had taken her that first time. The directness of her green gaze had clouded over, transforming her from sexy to vulnerable. And in that moment, he'd forgotten about her father, forgotten about his. There had been nothing but the whisper of pleasure skimming over his skin and the white heat building between them.

'We could do this with a bit more style, you know. Take some time,' he said.

'We don't *have* time.' Her voice was clipped. 'My father is binary in the way he approaches life. It's his way or no way. We need to present him with an irreversible fact—like a marriage certificate.' She met his gaze, her green eyes narrowing. 'I know this is a little basic, but unlike you I didn't have a couple of months to work everything out in detail. Shall we go in?'

The ceremony was short and functional.

The registrar, a pleasant woman in her fifties, spoke

her lines clearly, turning to each of them as she waited for their responses.

They had agreed to use English for the ceremony. But although they were both fluent, to her, the unfamiliar words made everything feel even more remote and pragmatic.

'Immacolata and Vicenzu, with your words today, I can now pronounce you husband and wife.' The woman smiled. 'And now you may seal the promises you have made with a kiss.'

Imma's expression didn't change, but Vicè felt her go still beside him. Glancing down, he saw that her green eyes were huge and over-bright, and her slim body was trembling like a wild flower in the wind.

It's just a kiss, he told himself.

And he lowered his head, assuming it would be nothing more than a passing brush of contact. But as their mouths touched he felt her lips part and instantly his body tensed, his insides tightening as a jolt of desire punched him in the gut.

Instinctively he slid his hand over her hip, tilting her face up to meet his and deepening the kiss.

Oh, but he hadn't meant to do that.

It was insane, stupid—beyond reckless—only he couldn't seem to stop himself.

He wanted her...wanted her with an urgency and intensity that was beyond his control.

He heard her breath hitch in her throat and was suddenly terrified that he would lose her—that he wouldn't be able to satisfy his hunger for her sweet, soft lips— but she didn't pull away.

Instead she leaned into him, her body moulding against his, and then he was pressing her closer, one hand sliding down her body, the other threading through her silky, dark hair.

His heart was pounding and his blood was surging through his limbs as an ache of need reared up inside him, pulsing and swelling, blotting out everything but the softness of her body.

From somewhere far away he heard a faint cough and, still fighting his drowning senses, he broke the kiss.

Imma was staring up at him, her green eyes unfocused, her lips trembling, and it was only the presence of the registrar and the two witnesses that stopped him from pulling her back into his arms and stripping that appalling dress off her body.

The registrar cleared her throat. 'Now, if you'd like to join me, we have the register here, all ready and waiting. Once that's signed, we're done.' She smiled. 'I'm sure you have plans for the rest of your special day.'

Vicè nodded. He did. But unfortunately for him, his marriage strictly forbade those plans being fulfilled.

Watching Imma sign the register, his shoulders tensed. It didn't matter that they had just come close to ripping off each other's clothes in public. Judging by the look on his new wife's face, that wasn't about to change any time soon.

Leaning back in her seat, Imma tilted her head sideways, gazing through the window at the cloudless blue sky. Her posture was determinedly casual, but her ears were on stalks and every five seconds or so her skin tightened and her stomach flipped up and over like a pancake in a skillet.

She felt on edge and distracted. And, even though

wild horses wouldn't have dragged it out of her, she knew she was waiting for Vicè to walk back into the cabin.

After the ceremony they had taken a taxi back to the private airfield, Vicè's hand still clamped around hers. But as soon as they had got on board the plane he had excused himself on the pretext of wanting to change into something less formal.

In reality, they had needed to give one another privacy to tell their respective families.

There was the sound of footsteps and instantly her nerves sent ripples of unease over her skin. But it was only the steward, Fedele, bringing a pot of coffee.

'Congratulations again, Signorina Buscetta—I mean Signora Trapani.' The steward smiled down at her. 'Would you like anything to go with your coffee? We have pastries and fruit.'

She shook her head. 'No, thank you, Fedele. But would you please thank the crew again for their kind words.'

It had been easy to tell the cabin crew that she was married, to receive their polite and no doubt genuine congratulations. Sharing the news with her father had been far less pleasant.

As predicted, Cesare had roared. For a good ten minutes he had threatened, reproached her, ranted and railed against her, his frustration and displeasure flowing unstoppably like lava from a volcano.

On any other day she would have tried to soothe him, to be the eye of calm at the centre of his storm.

But not today.

Maybe it had been the strain of the last few hours catching up with her, or perhaps she'd just been worried about letting the truth slip out, but she simply hadn't had it in her, so she had just let him rage until finally he'd registered her silence and said gruffly, 'So this Trapani boy—he loves you, does he?'

'Yes, Papà, he does.'

She'd heard her father grunt. 'And you love him?'

'I do—I really do.'

He'd sighed. 'Well, what's done is done. And if he makes you happy…'

It had been easier to lie than she had thought. Maybe it always was—maybe that was how her father managed to lie to her about Alessandro's business.

It hurt to think about all the other lies he might have told her. Only not as much as it had hurt having to stand next to Vicè at that dismal parody of a wedding and hear him repeat his vows knowing that he meant not one word of them.

She had heard him speaking, heard herself respond. She had watched the registrar smile and watched the witnesses sign the register. But she had felt totally numb, as though her veins had been filled with ice.

Until Vicè had kissed her.

Her heart bumped against her ribs as she remembered.

It had been as if he'd struck a match inside her. His mouth had tasted of freedom, and the warmth of his body against hers had seemed to offer danger and sanctuary all in one.

And just like that she had leaned into him, her body softening like wax touched by a flame. And all she knew was his closeness. And he had been all she wanted.

She shivered as a jolt of heat shot through her and

shifted in her seat, pressing her knees together, trying to ignore the flood of want.

Her cheeks felt hot. Yes, want. She wanted him.

Only how could she?

How could she still want Vicè after everything he had done? The lies he had told… The manipulation… The pretence…

But it didn't matter that it made no sense. It was the truth. And although she might be lying to her father, and to the cabin crew and to the rest of the world, she wasn't going to lie to herself.

The truth was that, even hating him as she did, with every fibre of her being, she still wanted him.

Kissing him should have been complicated.

Except it hadn't felt complicated.

It had been easy. Natural. Right. *Facile come bere un bicchiere d'acqua*, as her father liked to say when he was boasting about some deal he'd made.

But it was clearly just some kind of muscle memory kicking into action. It wouldn't happen again, of that she was certain. She might have been swept along in the moment, captivated by the swift, intoxicating intimacy of that kiss in an otherwise colourless ceremony, but—like the misplaced desire she had felt for Vicè yesterday—it had been just a blip.

'So how did it go? Am I going to be swimming with the fishes? Or did you manage to sweet talk him into accepting me as his son-in-law?'

A shadow fell across her face and, glancing up, she felt her pulse trip. Vicè was next to her, his dark eyes gazing down into her face, a mocking smile pulling at his mouth.

He was wearing a pair of jeans and a slim-fitting

navy T-shirt—the kind of low-key clothes that would make anyone else look ordinary. But Vicè didn't need logos or embellishments to draw the eye. His flawless looks and languid grace did that all on their own.

Dry-mouthed, she watched wordlessly, her heart lurching from side to side like a boat in a storm, as he dropped into the seat opposite her.

'It was fine. How about you?'

Ignoring her question, he picked up the coffee pot. 'How do you like it?' he murmured. 'Actually, no, don't tell me... I already know.'

Her stomach muscles trembled. She knew he was just talking about the coffee, but that didn't stop a slow, tingling warmth from sliding over her skin.

'I'm going to go with no milk and just a sprinkle of sugar.'

He held her gaze, his eyes reaching inside her so that for a moment she didn't even register what he'd said. Or that he was right.

Since agreeing to the terms of their marriage he'd been distant, cool, aloof... Sulking, presumably, at having the tables turned on him. Now, though, he seemed to have recovered his temper, and his dark gaze was lazily roaming her face. She knew it wasn't real but, try as she might, she couldn't stop herself—or her body anyway—from responding to him.

Annoyingly, she knew that he could sense her response and was enjoying it. The hairs on her arms rose. She had dictated the terms of their marriage. She was the one in control. So why did it feel as if he was playing with her?

Suddenly she wondered if she had done the right thing.

'Marianna told you,' she said quickly. She knew her face was flushed, and as he shook his head she frowned.

'She did not,' he said. His eyes hadn't left her mouth. 'But you're my wife, so I assume you want your coffee like your husband. Dark, firm-bodied, and with a hint of sweetness.'

He poured the coffee and held out a cup.

For a fraction of a second she hesitated, and then she took it. 'Thank you,' she said stiffly.

His eyes gleamed and, reaching across the table, he picked up his own cup. He seemed utterly at ease, and she wondered if he was still acting or if his mood really had changed.

It was impossible to tell. Up until a few days ago he'd been a stranger. Yet in the space of those few days so much had happened between them. Big, important, life-changing things.

'Sorry I took so long.' He lounged back in his chair, his dark lashes shielding the expression in his eyes. 'I needed to clear my mind. You know—' he made a sweeping gesture with his hand '—so much emotion after that wonderful ceremony. It was simple and yet so beautifully romantic.'

Hearing the mocking note in his voice, she gave him an icy glare. 'It's all you deserve.'

His gaze locked on hers. 'All I deserve?' He repeated her words softly. 'That's a missed opportunity.'

The glitter in his eyes made her nerves scream. 'What do you mean?'

Tilting his head back, he smiled slowly. 'Just that if I'd known you were trying to punish me I would have suggested something more exciting. Mutually satisfying.'

Her muscles tightened and she felt heat creep over

her cheeks. Stiffening her shoulders, she forced herself to look him in the eye. 'I wasn't trying to punish you. It was the only option under the circumstances. And I don't see why you even care about the ceremony anyway. You seduce virgins under false pretences. You don't do romance.'

Something flared in his eyes. 'I don't care, *cara*. But I can't believe a convent girl like you had that kind of ceremony pinned on her wedding board.'

Without warning he leaned forward and brushed her hair lightly with his fingertips. For a heartbeat she forgot to breathe. And then, as heat rushed through her body, she jerked backwards. 'What are you doing?'

'You have *coriandoli* in your hair,' he said softly, holding out his hand.

She gazed down at the rose petals, felt her pulse slowing. Vicè was wrong. She'd never planned her wedding day. In fact, she'd blocked it from her mind. Why would she want to plan a day that would so blatantly remind her that her life choices were not her own?

No, it had been Claudia—her sweet, overlooked little sister—who had dreamed of marriage and a husband and a home of her own.

Remembering her sister's tears, she curled her fingers into her palms. 'It's sweet of you to be concerned, Vicenzu,' she said. 'But I can have my dream wedding with my next husband.'

Vicenzu stared at her, her words resounding inside his head. *Seriously?* They had been married for less than two hours and she was already thinking about her next wedding? Her next husband?

His chest tightened. The thought of Imma being with

another man made him irrationally but intensely angry. And as his gaze roamed over her tight, taunting smile and the defiance in her green eyes, he felt his body respond to the challenge. To her beauty.

But his response wasn't just about the swing of her hair or the delicacy of her features—the dark, perfect curve of her eyebrows, the full, soft mouth, those arresting green eyes. There was something else…something hazy, elusive…a shielded quality.

Looking at her was like looking through a kaleidoscope: one twist and the whole picture shifted into something new, so that he couldn't imagine ever getting bored with her.

He felt his body harden. It had been a very long time since he'd got an erection from just *looking* at a woman.

Containing his temper, and the ache in his groin, he smiled back at her. 'But I'll always be your first, in so many ways, and that means something—don't you think?'

Watching colour suffuse her face, he knew he had got to her.

Leaning back in his seat, he glanced out of the window. 'So which godforsaken rock are we heading to now?' he asked tauntingly. 'Hopefully one with fewer monkeys and more beaches. I mean, this is our honeymoon, after all.'

'This is *not* our honeymoon.'

She leaned forward, her blush spreading over her collarbone, her narrowed green eyes revealing the depth of her irritation.

'This is business. We need to convince everyone, particularly our parents, that we are in love and that this marriage is real.'

Her mouth twisted.

'Otherwise you won't get your father's olive oil company back. And we both know that's all you're interested in.'

His pulse twitched. *Not true*. Right now he was extremely interested in whether the skin beneath the neckline of her dress was also flushed.

He forced his eyes to meet hers. Had she been inside his head on the flight over to Gibraltar, and in the car on the way to the register office, she would have found herself to be right. He had been furious at having lost the upper hand—having thrown it away, more like—and it had only been the thought of the family business that had kept him going.

Marriage to Imma was just a means to an end. In a year's time he would have his reward and he would have fulfilled his promise to Ciro. Vengeance would be his.

But a year was a long time. And right now, with Imma sitting so close, the business seemed less important than the way the pulse in her throat seemed to be leaping out at him through her skin.

'Fine...whatever.' He shrugged, lounging back and letting his arm droop over the back of his seat with a languid carelessness he didn't feel. 'But I meant what I said about monkeys and beaches.'

She gave him a look of exasperation.

'*Fine...whatever.* If it's such a big deal to you, then you can choose where we go.'

'Okay, then—let's go to Portofino. Let's go to my hotel.'

He'd spoken unthinkingly. The words had just appeared fully formed on his lips before he'd even realised what he was saying. Only now that he had said it, he knew that was what he wanted to do.

She was looking at him with a mixture of shock and confusion, as if he'd suddenly announced he wanted her to sleep in a bath of spaghetti. He felt nettled by her reaction.

For some inexplicable reason—maybe a desire to be on his home turf, or perhaps to prove there was a whole lot more to him than just a pretty face—he wanted her to see La Dolce Vita.

'Is that a problem?' he asked quietly.

But before she could reply, the steward appeared beside them.

'Signora Trapani—Chef would like to know if you're ready for lunch to be served?'

Imma nodded. 'Yes—*grazie*, Fedele.'

The steward began clearing the table.

'*Scusa*—I'm in the way. Here, let me move.'

Moving smoothly, Vicè swapped his seat for the one next to Imma. Taking advantage of Fedele's presence, he slid an arm around her waist, one hand snaking out to clasp hers firmly.

'That's better—isn't it, *cara*?'

She must have had a lot of practice in hiding her feelings, he thought, watching her lips curve into a smile of such sweetness that he almost forgot she was faking.

'You can let me go now,' she said quietly, her smile fading as Fedele disappeared.

'Why? He'll be back in a minute with lunch.'

He pulled her closer, tipping her onto his lap and drawing her against his chest. The sudden intimacy between them reminded him vividly of what had happened in her bedroom.

'Don't be scared, *cara...*' His heart was suddenly hammering inside his chest. 'This is just business...'

'I'm not scared,' she said hotly.

But she was scared. He could feel it in the way she was holding herself. Not scared of him, but of her response to him. Of this tingling insistent thread of need between them.

'Good,' he said softly. 'Because, as you so rightly pointed out, we need to convince everyone this is real—and that's not going to happen if we're sitting on opposite sides of the room. We need to practise making it look real.'

He stared down into her eyes.

'We need to act as if we can't keep our hands off one another. As if we want each other so badly it's like a craving. As if, even though it doesn't make sense, and it's never happened to us before and it's driving us crazy, we can't stop ourselves...'

That pretty much described how he'd been feeling ever since they'd met. How he was feeling right now, in fact. His blood was pounding in his ears and his body was painfully hard. He felt as though he was combusting inside.

Instinctively he lowered his face, sliding his hand into her hair.

'Vicè, stop—'

Stop? He hadn't even started!

Longing and fierce urgency rose up inside him, and as her fingers twitched against his chest it took every atom of willpower he had to stop himself from pressing his mouth to hers.

With an effort, he leaned back, smoothing all shades

of desire from his voice. 'So, are we going to Porto-fino, or not?'

There was a beat of silence, and then she nodded.

He kept his face still. 'I think ten days should be about right for a honeymoon. Or are you thinking longer...?'

'No.'

She shook her head, and he felt his stomach flip over at the sudden hoarseness in her voice.

'Ten days sounds perfect.'

Yes, it did, he thought, his body tensing as she slid off his lap.

Ten days.

And if he had his way every minute of all those days would be spent in bed...

CHAPTER SIX

IT WAS LATE afternoon by the time they arrived in Genoa. At the airport Vicè picked up his car—a surprisingly modest black convertible—and they drove south.

It wasn't just the modesty of his car that was surprising, Imma thought as they left the city's outskirts. Vicè was actually a good driver.

He was certainly nothing like her father. Cesare drove as he lived. Rushing forward aggressively and raging when he was forced to slow down or, worse still, stop.

Vicè drove with the same smooth, fluid grace as he did everything else.

She glanced over at him. They had barely spoken since setting off, but maybe that was a good thing. Every time they talked she seemed to start the conversation feeling in control but end it feeling he had the upper hand.

It didn't help that, despite everything she knew about him, her body persisted in overriding her brain whenever she was near to him.

Remembering exactly how near he had been earlier, on the plane, she felt a coil of heat spiral up inside her. She could tell herself it had been the plush intimacy of the plane or the glass of champagne that had affected her judgement. But it would be a lie to say she hadn't wanted him in that moment.

Only it was going to stop now. It had to.

This marriage might be a lie, but she couldn't lie to herself for a whole year.

She might have agreed theoretically with what Vicè had said on the plane, about making their marriage look real, but she knew she was going to find faking it far more difficult and painful than he would.

For him, those hours in her bed had been a necessary step in his plan to win back his father's business. A trick, a trap, a seduction.

For her, ignorant in her bliss, it had been something more.

He'd taught her about sex. About the sleek warmth of skin, the melting pleasure of touch and the decadent ache of climax.

It didn't matter that he'd been lying to her; her feelings for him had been real. And, even though she knew the truth now, the memory of how she had felt that night remained, overriding facts and common sense.

Admitting and accepting that would stop her repeating the reckless intimacy between them on the plane. But she needed to set some ground rules. Make it clear to him that she *would* play her part—but only in public, and only when absolutely necessary.

Feeling the car slow down, she glanced up ahead. The road was growing narrower and more winding. The palms of her hands were suddenly clammy.

Were they here?

As though he'd read her mind, Vicè turned towards

her and, taking one hand off the wheel, gestured casually towards the view through the windscreen.

'This is it. This is Portofino.'

She wasn't ready, she thought, her heart lurching. But it was too late. They were already cruising past pastel-coloured villas with dark green shutters, some strung with fluttering lines of laundry, others decorated with *trompe l'oeil* architectural flourishes that made her look twice.

The town centre was movie-set-perfect—a mix of insouciant vintage glamour and stealth wealth chic. Beneath the striped awnings of the cafes hugging the *piazzetta*, women in flowing, white dresses and men wearing linen and loafers lounged in the sunlight, talking and drinking Aperol spritz.

It was all so photogenic, so relaxed and carefree. A part of the world where *dolce far niente* was a way of life.

She swallowed, her throat suddenly dry. No wonder Vicè chose to live here. And now she would be living here too. Living here as Signora Trapani.

A shiver wound down her spine. Up until that moment she had been so focused on getting married she hadn't considered what being married would mean for her day-to-day life.

But here in Portofino, with Vicè, she would be free. For the first time ever there were no bodyguards tracking her every move, no Cesare dictating her agenda.

No rules to follow.

No rules at all.

Her stomach flipped over.

It was nerve-racking—like stepping from the safety of a ship onto new, uncharted land—and yet she wasn't scared so much as excited.

She let go of a breath. So much of her life had been spent feeling unsure about who she was, being scared to push back against the weight of duty and expectation. But without noticing she *had* pushed back, she realised with confusion. She had already changed, something shifting tectonically inside her.

How else could she be here with Vicè?

Her stomach knotted.

Much as she might want to flatter herself into believing that she had done so alone, incredibly—unbelievably— he was part of it. He had backed her into a corner and she had come out fighting. She had found another side of herself with him.

Feeling his gaze on the side of her face, she turned. 'It's beautiful,' she said simply.

His expression didn't alter, but she could sense he was pleased with her reaction.

'I'll save the guided tour for another time.'

His lip curved, and she felt his smile curl its way through her pelvis.

'I'm sure you'll be wanting to get out of those clothes.'

Refusing to take the bait, she lifted her chin. 'So what happens at the hotel?'

Shifting in his seat, he changed gear, his smile twitching at the corners of his mouth. 'Well, there are people who come and stay and use the rooms—I call them guests—'

She clenched her jaw. 'I meant what's the plan for us?'

'Relax, *cara*.' He was grinning now. 'We'll just play it by ear.'

'That's not a plan,' she snapped.

Back on the plane, she had told herself that it was a

good idea to come here. La Dolce Vita was a magnet for Hollywood actors, rock stars and rappers, so there was bound to be a bunch of paparazzi hanging around the hotel. Obviously they would be hot news for a couple of days, but it would all die down pretty quickly and then their lives could go back to normal.

'Normal' with the occasional necessary public display of affection.

Now, though, she was starting to see flaws in the plan—the major one being that Vicè didn't appear to have a plan.

'It'll be fine,' he said.

They were heading up a hill now, along a road edged with cypress trees and pines. Away from the town it was quieter, the air heavy with the scent of honeysuckle and lemon trees, and there was a surprising lushness to the greenery around them.

She felt the car slow again, her heartbeat accelerating as he turned between two scuffed pillars.

'Don't worry—I can do all the talking.'

He made it sound so easy. But then, of course, he was good at painting castles in the air.

Remembering how effortlessly he had persuaded her to believe in him, she gritted her teeth. 'As long as you keep to the script and don't contradict me—'

'Spoken like a true wife,' he said softly, stopping the car. Pulling off his sunglasses, he glanced over his shoulder. 'We're here.'

Her heart gave a startled leap and, blinking into the sunlight, Imma looked up and felt her mouth drop open. She'd seen photos, but nothing did justice to the building in front of her.

Surrounded by palm trees, flecked with sunlight, the

peaches-and-cream-coloured hotel oozed Italian Riviera style. But this was more than just a playground for
VIPs, she thought, watching a flurry of petals flutter
down from the wisteria-draped facade. It was magical,
and the knowledge that Vicè was the man behind the
magic made her heart hammer in her ears.

She jumped slightly as Vicè opened her door.

'It used to be a monastery, would you believe?'

He gave her one of his pulse-fluttering smiles and she
bit her lip. In this mood he was impossible to resist—
just like the hand he was holding out to her.

'No, I wouldn't.'

His fingers threaded through hers and she stepped
out of the car, her muscles tightening as he slid an arm
around her waist.

'It's true. The monks kept getting overrun by pirates,
so they abandoned it. Moved further inland.'

'What happened to the pirates?'

'Oh, they're still here.' He smiled, his dark eyes glittering in the early-evening sunlight. 'One of them, anyway.'

The heat of his body matched the heat in his eyes.
For a moment he stared down at her, and the pull between them she'd been trying so hard to ignore flared
to life inside her.

'*Ehi, capo!* You're back!'

Swinging round, Vicè raised his hand, his smile widening as a young man with streaked blond hair, sleepy brown
eyes and an equally wide smile strode towards them.

'Matteo. *Ciao!*'

'I was expecting you two days ago.'

'What can I say? I got distracted.'

As the two men embraced Imma watched in confusion.

Capo? Was Vicè his *boss*?

She tried and failed to picture any of her father's employees talking to Cesare in such a casual, effusive manner. But all she could think about were those emails she had read and his treatment of Alessandro.

She felt her stomach clench. She still wasn't ready to go there, and she was almost grateful when Vicè turned towards her, reaching out for her hand.

'Come here, *cara*.'

He pulled her closer, his dark gaze on her face.

'This beautiful woman is the reason I got distracted. Imma, this is Matteo, the hotel manager here and a good friend. Matteo—this is Imma, my wife.'

Her pulse jumped. Vicè was looking at her—really looking at her—so that it felt as if he was reaching inside of her, claiming her for his own.

'My wife,' he repeated softly.

It was an act, she told herself. It was all for show. Only she couldn't stop her stomach from turning over in an uncontrollable response to the intimacy of his words and the flame in his eyes.

For a split second time seemed to end. Just stop.

She forgot where she was and why she was even there. Around her the air seemed to thicken into an invisible wall, and inside the wall was Vicè, his skin dappled with sunlight, his dark gaze pulling her closer...

'You got married!'

She blinked as Matteo grabbed Vicè in a one-armed hug.

'*Che bello!* That's fantastic news. I'm so pleased for you both.'

'Thank you, bro. It was all a bit *di impulso*.' Glancing over at Imma, he grinned. 'What can I say? She swept me off my feet.'

Imma forced her mouth into a smile. Vicè made it all sound so plausible—no wonder Matteo was beaming at them in delight. But his congratulations were warm and genuine, and it felt wrong accepting them under such false pretences.

She felt a flash of anger. How was she going to do this for a whole year? Smile and lie to every single person she met? It was a daunting prospect, and the wider implications of what she'd agreed to do made her heart cramp.

She felt Vicè's hand tighten around hers.

'Matteo, can you get the bags brought round?'

'Sure, boss.'

'Come on.'

He turned and, still holding her hand, led her away from the hotel to a narrow path that disappeared into the lush undergrowth.

'I'll show you to the villa.'

She let him lead her between the citrus trees and beneath the boughs of myrtle and laurel, but as soon as they were out of sight she jerked her hand away.

'That's enough,' she snapped.

Vicè stopped. His pulse was racing.

In that moment when he and Imma had been talking to Matteo he'd forgotten that their marriage wasn't real. More confusingly, watching her face soften, he'd wanted it to be real.

Pulse slowing, he thought back to when he'd agreed to marry her. At the time he'd been too stunned by her conditions, too determined to get back his father's business, to think about what it would mean to live this particular lie. He'd been lying for so long, to so many people, why would one more matter?

Except now it did.

He wanted to stop, to erase the past and start again.

And not just his marriage to Imma. He wanted to go back—way, way back, to before his father's death—and live his whole life differently.

He turned to face her, his expression benign, one eyebrow raised questioningly. 'Enough what?'

'I don't want you touching me,' she snapped.

'Really?' he said, one eyebrow raised sceptically. 'You didn't seem to have any objections on the plane. You know, when you were sitting on my lap...'

Watching the pink flush rise over her face up to her hairline, Vicè held his breath. Was it embarrassment or desire? Maybe it was embarrassment at her desire?

Briefly he wondered what she would do if he pulled her closer and kissed her. Kissed her until she melted into him and she was his again. Beneath the overhanging greenery, he saw her eyes had darkened but, glancing over at her taut, flushed face, he pushed back against the heat rising like a wave inside his body.

Sadly this wasn't the right time or place.

'In fact, things seemed to be getting quite...*cosy.*' He drew the word out, elongating it deliberately until the colour in her cheeks grew darker.

She ignored his remark and, tipping her head back in the manner of a queen addressing a commoner, she gave him a glacial stare. 'Are you going to show me where we're going or do I have to find my own way?'

He sighed. 'Isn't it a little early in our married life

to start with the nagging, *cara*? Could we at least get to our one-week anniversary first?'

Whistling softly, he sidestepped, moving past her furious face.

Coming to Portofino had been a whim. But, watching her reaction as they'd pulled up in front of the hotel, he had felt his stomach grow warm. She had obviously been expecting some seedy 'no-tell motel', but he could tell she was surprised. And impressed.

He breathed in on a rush of pleasure. Was it impressive? He tried to see it through her eyes.

To himself, and to everyone else too—especially his family—he'd always downplayed how much he cared about the Dolce, making out that it was more of a hobby than a business so nobody would suspect that it mattered to him. But Imma's open-mouthed wonder made him want to stop pretending and tell her how he really felt.

At the villa, he unlocked the door, feeling the usual rush of conflicting emotions.

He loved the spacious rooms. The polished hardwood floors, high ceilings and antique Murano chandeliers all captured the glamour of a bygone era, and the tall windows caught the gentle sea breeze and offered mesmerising views of the serene cerulean bay.

It was the perfect backdrop for his *dolce far niente* lifestyle. But it was not home. Home would only ever be his family's estate in Sicily.

Turning, he found Imma standing at the entrance, one foot over the threshold. He felt his breath catch. With her dark hair tumbling over her shoulders, and anger mingling with apprehension in her green eyes, she looked some like a woodland nymph who had stumbled across a hunter.

It took him a moment to realise that he was the hunter. Another to realise that he didn't like how that made him feel.

He felt something pinch inside his chest. Revenge was supposed to be sweet, but he hated the guarded expression on her face—*and* knowing that he was the cause of it.

'Okay, this is it. I'll give you a tour of the house first, and then we can just chill for a bit. Maybe have an *aperitivo* and then—'

Distracted by the various and all equally tempting versions of 'and then' playing out inside his head, he broke off from what he was saying and headed towards the kitchen.

He kept the tour brief and factual, opening doors and listing rooms.

'That's it for this level.' He gestured towards the staircase. 'Shall we?'

For a moment she stared warily back at him, as though he was Bluebeard, inviting her to see where he kept his other wives, and then, averting her gaze, she stepped past him. His chest tightened first and his groin next, as he caught the scent of her perfume, and he took a moment to steady himself before following her upstairs.

'There are no guest rooms,' he said. 'Not that we need any.' He gave her a slow, teasing smile. 'Guests on a honeymoon would be a little de trop, don't you think, *cara*?'

'Not on this one,' she said sweetly.

Touché, he thought, holding her gaze. He liked it that

he could get under her skin—metaphorically speaking. Of course, what he'd like more would be to actually strip her naked and lick every centimetre of her smooth, satiny body.

They had reached the top of the stairs.

The large, beautiful bedroom stretched the whole length of this floor, and it was filled with light and the scent from the honeysuckle that grew prolifically in the gardens below. Strangely, though, he could still smell Imma's perfume.

He watched as she stopped and turned slowly on the spot, stilling as she caught sight of their bags sitting side by side at the end of the bed.

'What did you say about the other bedrooms?'

'There are none.'

Catching sight of the vibrant aquamarine sea, he walked towards the French windows and opened them, blinking into the sunlight as he stepped onto the balcony.

'You know, sometimes you can see dolphins swimming in the bay. When the Romans came here there were so many of them they named it Portus Delphini—that's why it's called Portofino.'

Imma came and stood beside him. She was frowning.

'Say that again?'

'Portus Delphini—it means Port of the Dolphins—'

'I meant about the bedrooms.'

He dropped onto one of the chairs that were scattered casually around the balcony, extending his legs and stretching his arms above his head. He was fully aware that she was watching him, waiting for his reply, and the tension in her body made his own body grow taut.

'Oh, that…' he said casually. 'I said this is the only one. This is *our* bedroom.'

'No.' She shook her head, her green eyes narrowing. 'This is *your* bedroom. I will take a room at the hotel.'

Now he frowned. 'At the hotel? How is that going to work?'

She was looking at him as if she wanted to take off her shoes and throw them at his head.

'Very simply. You sleep *here*. I sleep *there*.'

He shook his head. 'You're not making sense, *cara*. We're supposed to be crazily in love. People who are crazily in love don't sleep in separate beds—never mind separate rooms in a different building.'

Eyes narrowing, she put her hands on her hips. 'But we're not in love, Vicè.'

Her voice was tense, and he heard the depth of her hurt and anger.

'Oh, I'm sorry—did you start to believe your own lies? I suppose that's what happens when you never tell the truth.'

His jaw tightened. 'You don't get to lecture me about the truth. Not after that show you put on in *your* bedroom the other night.'

For a moment he thought she was going to slap him again and knew on some level he would deserve it. Knew also that he didn't like this version of himself. Worse, he knew his father would be appalled. Alessandro had been a *gentiluomo*. He had treated everyone with the same quiet courtesy, but had reserved a special respectful tenderness for his wife.

'At least it was only one night,' she said acidly. 'Your whole *life* is a show, Vicè.'

Her blunt words felt like the waves that battered the coastline during winter storms.

He stared at her in silence.

Probably ninety-nine percent of what was written about him was untrue, or at best vaguely based on the truth, but he never bothered demanding a retraction. There was no point. His 'bad' reputation was good for business. And, as Ciro's brother, he had grown so used to unfavourable comparisons that he hardly registered them or even knew how to resent them.

But this woman seemed to know exactly which buttons to press. She made him feel things—good and bad—that no one ever had before. Somehow she'd sneaked under the barriers he'd built against the world, so that he was finding it harder and harder to maintain his usual couldn't-care-less attitude.

With an effort, he tethered his temper. 'I'm well aware we're not in love. But what matters is that we appear to be.'

'In public,' she countered. 'Look, we made an agreement—'

'Yes, we did,' he agreed. 'It's called marriage.'

Her chin jutted forward. 'A marriage that I made clear would not include our sleeping together.'

He shrugged. 'Okay, so go back to your father,' he said.

It was an idle threat. She had already made it clear that was not an option. But as her eyes darted towards the staircase he felt his heart jolt, his mind tracking back to the way she'd looked at him when Matteo had been there.

Her smile had felt like the sun breaking over this balcony in the afternoon. Warm and irresistible and real.

He didn't want her to leave.

In fact, he was determined that she should stay.

Obviously he wanted her to stay, or he wouldn't get his father's business back, but for some reason that seemed to matter less than getting her to share that soft, sweet smile with him in private.

'Let him find you another husband,' he said softly. 'Shouldn't be a problem. There must be a queue of men wanting to marry a woman who walked out on her wedding night. And, if not, I'm sure your *papà* will persuade someone to step up.'

Watching the colour leave her face, he knew she was cornered.

'You did this on purpose—didn't you?' she prompted, her incredible green eyes flashing with anger and resentment. 'You knew there was only one bedroom. That's why you wanted to come here.'

'Me? I'm just a passenger, *cara*,' he said disingenuously. 'This is your itinerary. I go where you tell me.'

Her green eyes flared. 'Well, in that case, you can go to hell!'

'Maybe later.' He glanced at his watch. 'Right now, we need to get ready.'

'For what?'

'We have dinner plans. At the hotel.'

Was he being serious?

Imma gaped at him. They were in the middle of an argument—*no*, scratch that, they were in the middle of a power struggle—and he wanted them to just wrap it up and have dinner together.

As if!

Fury rose up inside her and, lifting her chin, she folded her arms. 'I'm not feeling hungry.'

His eyes met hers, and the sudden dark intensity of his gaze made her breath stall in her throat.

'Oh, I wouldn't worry... I'm sure I can find something on the menu to prick your appetite,' he said softly.

The air between them seemed to thicken, his words making her heart miss a beat in such a maddening and all too predictable way that she wanted to scream. He'd tricked her into coming here. He was vile. Manipulative. Duplicitous.

So why was her stupid body betraying her like this?

Her pulse jolted as he began unbuttoning his shirt.

'What are you doing?'

'Getting changed.' Catching sight of her face, he sighed. 'We have to eat. Well, I do, anyway. And we're going to have to face people sooner or later. So let's get it over with. We'll show our faces, smile, look loved up and then it's done.'

'Fine. Since you put it so nicely,' she said stiffly. 'But just because I'm going to dinner with you it doesn't change anything.'

He looked at her for a long moment. Probably it was a new experience for him. No doubt most women would move continents to have dinner with Vicenzu Trapani.

'Of course not,' he murmured. 'The bathroom's through there. I'll see you downstairs.' His dark eyes met hers, then dropped to her mouth, then lower still. 'Call me if you need me to zip you up. Or, better still, unzip you. I'll be happy to help.'

In the bathroom, she washed quickly and changed out of her dress.

How had this happened? At home, when she wanted

space, she'd run a bath and lie back, closing her eyes and losing herself in the steam and the silence. And now she was here, hiding in another bathroom from another man.

Only wasn't that the reason she had agreed to marry Vicè? To change all that? To be someone different?

It wasn't the only reason.

Her pulse twitched. Did he know the effect he had on her?

Of course.

Vicè was an expert on women—he knew exactly what to look for. He probably thought he had her all worked out, and that when he clicked his fingers she would come running. But he didn't know her at all.

She glanced down at her dress, her pulse beating unevenly. It was new. Her sister had chosen it for her on a shopping trip in Milan. It had been a rare day of freedom for them. Her mouth twisted. Freedom that had included a posse of bodyguards, of course.

She'd been planning to wear it at the evening function after Claudia's wedding. Only in the end she hadn't had the guts to put it on in front of her father.

Glancing down, she felt her skin tighten. The dress was green, a shade brighter than her eyes, and to say that it was 'fitted' was an understatement. Had it looked this clinging in the shop? Probably. But after two glasses of Prosecco she hadn't noticed or cared.

It wasn't her usual style, any more than the black patent skyscraper heels were. But her sister was always wanting her to dress up, and she'd been so excited, so eager for Imma to buy it.

She lifted her chin and met the gaze of her reflection.

She would wear it tonight—for Claudia—and prove to Vicenzu that he knew nothing about her at all.

But as she walked downstairs her bravado began to falter with every step.

Catching sight of him standing with his back to her, his eyes fixed on the sunset lighting up the bay, she felt a rush of panic. Perhaps she should change.

But before she had a chance to retreat he turned and her heart lurched. Suddenly she wasn't thinking about what she was wearing any more. She was too busy marvelling at his blatant masculine beauty.

He was wearing black trousers, a dark grey polo shirt and loafers, and she liked how he looked. *A lot*.

Her throat tightened. She liked how he was looking at her even more.

'Is it too much?' she asked quickly as his dark gaze skimmed her body.

'Not at all.' He hesitated, then took a step forward. 'It suits you.'

His voice was cool, and she wasn't sure what he meant by that remark, but she didn't want to get inside his head to find out. Right now she just wanted to go somewhere, anywhere there were other people—people who would prevent her from doing something stupid.

Even more stupid than marrying him.

Maybe he felt the same way. Or perhaps he was just desperate for company, she thought as he escorted her swiftly and purposefully towards the hotel.

They entered through a side door. 'We'll deal with the paps later,' Vicè said, his hand locking with hers.

It was lucky for him that he was holding her hand so tightly, otherwise she would have scuttled back to the villa. Even without the paparazzi, the experience of walking into this hotel was intimidating. The beautiful decor was the embodiment of relaxed chic, a perfect mix of retro glamour and contemporary cool, but it was still overshadowed by the fame of the guests.

In the space of a minute she counted at least five A-list film stars, two motor racing drivers, a tennis champion and a disgraced former Italian prime minister—and all of them seemed to know Vicè and wanted to offer their congratulations. Even those who didn't were nearly falling over to catch a glimpse of him.

'They're bored with me,' he murmured.

'What?' She glanced up at him in confusion.

'It's you they've come to see.'

Wrong, she thought as they sat down at their table in the restaurant. He was so devastating you could gaze at him for several lifetimes and not get bored.

He was a gracious, natural host, and a master of *sprezzatura*—that ability to make things happen seemingly without effort or any apparent thought. And he liked people…accepted them for who they were.

Watching him stop to speak to a middle-aged couple who were celebrating their wedding anniversary, she felt her pulse slow. Vicè was turning out to be an enigma. And, even though she knew that feeling this way wasn't clever, he was a mystery she found herself wanting to solve.

The view from the panoramic terrace was legendary, and she could see why. In the fading light of the setting sun the curve of the town's pastel-coloured houses looked like something from a dream.

But if the view was enchanting, the food was sublime. She chose *paté di seppia* followed by *zembi au pesto* and savoured every mouthful.

'So you've found your appetite?'

Looking up, Imma blushed.

'It's fine,' he assured her. Leaning forward, he took her hand. 'It's been a long day. You need to eat.'

Watching him kiss her hand, she wondered if it would feel different if he meant it. 'The food is delicious,' she said.

'I'm glad you like it.'

She met his gaze. 'I didn't think it would be so…'

'So what?'

His expression hadn't changed, but she could sense the tension around his eyes.

'So magical here. You've made something remarkable, and you've done it on your own. Your family must be very proud.'

He nodded. 'Of course.'

'So why did you choose Portofino?'

He shrugged. 'I didn't. It chose me.'

It was a perfectly reasonable reply, but she couldn't shift the feeling that there was more to it than what he was saying. But if there was, he wasn't sharing it. He talked easily and amusingly about anything and everything except himself. Then he either made a joke or changed the subject.

When the meal was over Vicè caught her hand.

'Let's get this done.' He eyed her sideways. 'You know we're going to have to kiss? Nothing beyond the call of duty—just enough to make it look real. Are you okay with that?'

She nodded. 'For the cameras, yes.'

She had been expecting a couple of photographers,

but as they walked down the steps of the hotel a crowd of paparazzi rushed forward.

'Vicè, is it true you two only met twenty-four hours ago?'

'Give me a break. I'm good—but not that good.' He grinned. 'It was at least forty-eight.'

There were yells of laughter.

'Aren't you going to kiss your wife, Vicè?'

Her heart leapt as he turned and looked down at her.

'I think I should,' he said softly, his eyes dropping to her mouth.

His hand moved to her back. She felt her stomach disappear as he tipped her head back and stared into her eyes, and then he leaned forward and kissed her.

It was the lightest of kisses, fleeting and gentle. But, staring up into his dark eyes, she felt her brain freeze and her body begin to melt. Pulse jumping, she leaned into him and pressed her mouth against his.

For a fraction of a second she felt his surprise, and then his hand caught in her hair and he was pulling her closer. Her head spun. She could taste his hunger…feel her own hunger flowering with a swiftness that shocked her. Blood was roaring in her ears.

Her fingers slid over his chest, curling into the fabric of his shirt, and she couldn't stop herself from slanting her body against his.

His lips were still moving slowly, deliberately over hers, drawing out the heat that was tightening her stomach so that she was shivering, shaking inside, her body melting with a raw hunger that was as torturous as it was exquisite. And then she was kissing him back, fusing her mouth with his.

The roar of the photographers' voices filled her head.

For a few moments the world turned white. Then she felt his swift indrawn breath, and as he lifted his head she dimly became aware of her surroundings again.

'Okay, that's it for now.' Vicè smiled, and seconds later he was leading her back down the path to his villa.

Her heart was hammering against her ribs and her cheeks felt scalded. It had been supposed to be for show, but as he'd drawn her into the half-circle of his arms she had never wanted anything to be more real.

Had Vicè sensed her unbidden response beneath the performance? The thought made her throat tighten and as they walked into the villa she spun round to face him. 'I can't believe you just did that.'

He arched an eyebrow. 'What did you expect? A peck on the cheek?'

Her voice was shaking. 'That kiss was *way* "beyond the call of duty"!'

And she had kissed him back. Her teeth clenched. She was furious with herself. But to reveal that would reveal her vulnerability, and so, as he dropped down onto the sofa, she directed her anger towards him.

'You love this, don't you? Playing your stupid games—'

His eyes narrowed, and then he was on his feet and moving towards her so fast that she only just had time to throw up a defensive hand.

'*Me* playing games?' He shook his head, an incredulous look on his handsome face. 'I'm not the one playing games here, Imma.'

'What is that supposed to mean?' she hissed.

'It means all this fighting and flirting. You *do* know that eventually we're going to end up back where we started? Naked. In bed.'

Her eyes clashed with his. 'In your dreams.'

'In yours too,' he taunted.

His words made her breathing jerk. She shook her head in denial. 'You are impossibly arrogant.'

'So I've been told. But that doesn't change the facts—which are that you want me as much as I want you. So why don't we skip the fighting and go straight to the sex?'

Cheeks flaming, she stared up at him angrily, the truth of his words only intensifying her need to deny them.

'You didn't want me before—you wanted your father's business. And you only want me now because you can't risk having an affair and blowing our deal. As to what I want—do you really think I'd sleep with you again after everything that's happened?'

'Why not?'

His eyes were fixed on her face, hot and dark, and as she caught the intense heat in them her body began to tremble.

'We're adults. We're both getting what we want from this arrangement. Except each other. But I'm willing to forget the past if you are.'

Forget the past.

For a second she couldn't trust herself to speak. 'Excuse me.' She stepped past him.

He frowned. 'Where are you going?'

'To get some bedding. I'm going to sleep on the sofa.'

For a moment he clearly thought she was joking, and then he swore softly. 'Fine. I'll sleep down here.'

She stumbled slightly, caught off guard by his sudden acquiescence.

'Fine. And, just so you know, from now until we leave, there won't be any more public appearances for the two of us. Show's over, Vicè.'

CHAPTER SEVEN

Rolling onto his back, Vicè savagely punched the pillow behind his head and gazed up at the ceiling.

Newsflash: this sofa might look great, and lounging on it with a Negroni was fine, but it was definitely not designed for sleep.

Not that he was going to sleep any time soon, he thought. Even if his neck hadn't been in agony, his body was wound so tightly he doubted he would ever sleep again. In fact, it had been on high alert ever since Imma had sashayed downstairs earlier and he'd forgotten to breathe.

Gone had been the absurdly staid mother-of-the-bride navy dress and in its place had been a silk number the colour of absinthe that had clung to her body without a ripple, exposing her slim curves and shimmering biscotti-coloured skin.

And then there had been those shoes…

A muscle pulsed in his jaw. It was a toss-up as to whether that dress or her parting shot had rendered him more speechless.

Remembering Imma's words, he felt his muscles tighten.

Show's over.

Wrong, he thought. It wasn't over. This was just an intermission.

Scowling, he shifted onto his side. Just an intermission that was longer than necessary and extremely uncomfortable.

He scowled. How had he ended up here? Spending a night on the sofa while his new wife slept alone in *his* bed?

He couldn't work out what had happened. So he might not be a business tycoon like Ciro, or even his father, but if there was one thing he understood above all others it was women.

He gritted his teeth. Make that all women except Imma.

Take tonight: she had been spitting fire over their sleeping arrangements, storming off into the bathroom when he'd told her about their dinner reservation. But then she'd seemed to calm down and relax over dinner, eating and enjoying her meal even though she'd claimed earlier she had no appetite.

Her mood had shifted a little when they'd walked out of the hotel. She had been jittery—understandably. Like oysters, the paparazzi were an acquired taste. And, unlike him, Imma had very little experience of facing a phalanx of photographers. But he'd warned her that they would have to perform for the cameras and she'd seemed to be up for it.

His pulse began to beat thickly in his blood.

Had he meant to kiss her like that? As if a clock had been counting down to the end of the world and only by kissing her could he stop time and stay alive?

No, he hadn't—and he hadn't expected her to respond like that either.

He'd thought she would play coy, do her 'duty'...

But then she'd leaned into him, her lips parting. And, lost in the sweetness of her mouth and the pliant heat of her body, he had kissed her back.

His groin tightened at the memory.

It had not been a duty kiss. But, *mannaggia alla miseria*, he was only human, and when a beautiful woman was in his arms, kissing him, what was he supposed to do?

He felt his shoulders tense. She thought he'd planned it—that it had been yet another example of him lying to her about his intentions. The truth was that his arousal had been so fast, so intense, he'd lost the ability to think, much less contemplate all possible interpretations of his actions.

In the time it had taken for her to part her lips he'd forgotten about the paparazzi, forgotten their marriage wasn't real. His breath, his body, his whole being, had been focused on the feel of her mouth on his and he had been powerless to stop.

Only there was no way to prove that to her. Not that she would believe him anyway. And could he really blame her?

His chest tightened. Never before had he treated anyone quite so unfairly as he'd treated Imma.

He'd lied to her repeatedly and manipulated her, using every smile and glittering gaze in his repertoire to lure her away from her family and seduce her. Of course she wouldn't believe him.

Sighing, he stared across the darkened living room.

And that was why he would be sleeping on this sofa for the foreseeable future. Or rather *not* sleeping.

He sat up. There was no point in just lying there.

Glancing out of the window, he caught sight of a flicker of light reflected from the surface of the pool and felt a rush of relief, as if someone had thrown him a life jacket. A swim was just what he needed to clear his head and cool his body.

Outside, the warm air clung to his skin. For a moment he stood on the edge of the pool and then, tipping forward, he executed a flawless dive into the water.

For the next forty minutes or so he swam lengths, until his chest and legs ached in unison. Turning over, he floated on his back, his lungs burning.

A huge pale moon hung over the sea, and above him the inky blue-black sky was crowded with stars. The air was heavy with the scent of cypress and honeysuckle and vibrated with the hum of cicadas. It was all impossibly romantic—the perfect setting, in fact, for a wedding night.

All that was missing was his beautiful bride.

He was back where he started.

Grimacing, he turned towards the pool's edge, his limbs stretching through the water. As he pulled himself out and draped a towel around his neck, a tiny speckled lizard darted between the shadows.

But that wasn't what made him catch his breath.

Beyond the shadows, her green dress luminous in the moonlight, her long dark hair hanging loosely over her shoulders, was his wife.

Imma felt her body tense.

Upstairs in the bedroom she had felt trapped. The windows on to the balcony had been open to the sea breeze, but still she had felt hot and panicky.

Back on Pantelleria, marrying Vicè had seemed like

a good idea. She had thought she needed time and space to deal with the consequences of her actions—and his. She'd also naively believed that she could play him at his own game.

But the truth, as she'd so humiliatingly discovered this evening, was that she was out of her depth and floundering.

He was too slick, too good at twisting words and situations to his advantage. And for someone who was so poor at telling the truth he was remarkably good at pointing out dishonesty and hypocrisy in other people—namely herself.

She had known that sleep was beyond her, so she hadn't bothered to undress. Instead she had slipped off her shoes and tried to rest.

Even that, though, had been impossible.

How could she rest in his room? On his bed? And it *was* his bed. She'd been able to smell him. His aftershave and something else…a scent that had made her stomach grow warm and her head swim. Clean, masculine…like salt or newly chopped wood. She had felt it slipping over her face like a veil.

Veil. Her throat had closed around the word like a vice.

With Vicè's denials and accusations still echoing in her head, she had forgotten that this was supposed to be her wedding night.

Some wedding night.

She had never felt more alone, so she had crept downstairs, past the sofa, and gone out into the heavy night air.

She had thought Vicè would be asleep. But he was

not only very much awake, he was standing in front of her. In boxer shorts. Extremely wet boxer shorts.

Her stomach flipped over and for a heartbeat she couldn't move. She no longer seemed to know how to make her legs work. But she did know that no good would come of her staying there.

'Imma. Please, wait—'

Against her will, against every instinct she had, she made her body still. With an effort, she turned to face him. 'Why? So you can make me feel stupid? You don't need to bother, Vicè. Really. I'm already doing a great job of that all on my own.'

He took a step towards her. 'I don't want to make you feel stupid. I just want to talk.'

She looked away, swallowing against the ache in her throat, feeling trapped again. 'Well, that's a lovely idea, but we don't talk. We argue. And I'm tired of arguing.'

'We do talk,' he said quietly. 'That first night at your father's villa we talked a lot.'

She stared at him in confusion. But he was right. They had talked that night about lots of things. Actually, *she* had talked—and that in itself was remarkable.

Usually, she was the listener. When it was just the two of them, Claudia would always be the one chattering on about some recipe she was going to try, and at work, with her father's shadow looming large over everything, her opinions were politely ignored. As for Cesare himself—like most rich, powerful men, he was far too convinced of his own rightness to invite other viewpoints.

A lump of misery swelled inside her. She was getting distracted. *At her father's villa, Vicè had a reason to listen to her.*

'That wasn't real,' she said flatly. 'None of this is real.'

'I am—and you are.' His eyes held hers. 'And so is this thing between us.'

She shook her head. 'There *is* no thing between us, Vicè.'

But of their own accord her eyes fixed on his chest. For a few half seconds she stared at the drops of water trickling down over his smooth golden skin, and then she looked away, her breathing ragged, her denial echoing hollowly around the empty terrace.

She had taken him back to her father's villa thinking that one night with him would give her the answers she needed. Instead it had simply raised more questions. Like what kind of woman could still want a man like him? And how—*where*—was she ever going to find another man who would override the memory of his touch, his kiss?

'Even if there is, we're not going to do anything about it.'

His eyes were steady and unblinking. 'We already have. So why are you still denying how we both feel?'

'Because it doesn't make any sense,' she mumbled.

'Does it have to?'

She looked up at him, made mute by the directness of his words and the complicity they implied.

He was silent for a moment, and then he sighed. 'Look, Imma, I don't want to argue any more than you do, so could we call a truce? Please?'

Her heart contracted. 'Forget the past, you mean?'

He stared at her. 'Not forget it—just put it on hold.'

She frowned. 'We're not talking about a nuisance call. This is my sister's life—her heart.' *My heart.* Her eyes were filling with tears. 'She doesn't deserve what your brother has done to her.'

'Oh? But my father *did* deserve to be hounded in the last few months of his life?'

His voice was suddenly hard, his eyes even harder. *So much for a truce*, she thought.

'And my mother? She deserved to lose her home? Her husband?'

His tone made her shiver.

'Of course not.' She hesitated. 'Is that why you want the business back? For her?'

For a moment he seemed confused, as though he didn't understand her words.

'I want my father back—so does my mother. There's only one reason I want the business, and one reason I want you as my wife—and that's so your father gets a taste of his own medicine.'

She flinched, the scorn in his voice biting into her flesh. This was exactly why she should have turned and walked away when she'd had the chance.

There was a tense, expectant silence, and then Vicè ran a hand over his face.

'I didn't mean that.' He was breathing unevenly. 'What I said about wanting you… I was angry—I *am* angry—but I don't want to hurt you.'

Glancing up, she tensed. His eyes were filled with a kind of bewildered frustration. He was hurting, and his pain cut through her own misery.

Without thinking, she reached out and touched his arm. 'I wish my father hadn't acted like he did, and if I could go back and change one thing in all of this it would be that.'

There was a silence. He stared at her, but he didn't shake off her hand.

After a moment, he said slowly, 'Not what happened between us? You wouldn't go back and change that?'

He sounded confused, disbelieving, and his dark eyes were searching her face as though he was trying to read her thoughts.

Her mind turned over her words. She was suddenly confused herself. But it hadn't occurred to her to regret that night they'd shared. She wouldn't exchange those beautiful, sensual hours in Vicè's arms for anything. And it hadn't been just the heat and the hunger, or even the fact that for those few short hours she had believed he wanted her for herself.

That night with him had been the first time she had consciously defied her father's wishes—not to his face, maybe, but it had felt like it. The first time she had made decisions about her own life.

'No, I wouldn't change that,' she said quietly.

'I wouldn't change it either.'

His eyes held hers and, catching the heat in his dark gaze, she felt a rush of panic. Last time she had willingly walked into the fire. But she couldn't do so again, knowing what she did now.

'I can't do this,' she said. And this time she acted, turning and running swiftly back into the house.

He caught up with her in the living room, his body blocking her escape. 'Where are you going?'

'Anywhere you're not.' She spoke breathlessly.

'For a year?' He looked and sounded incredulous. 'You're going to keep running away from me for a whole year?'

'I'm not like you, Vicenzu. I can't just switch it on and off for the cameras.'

'What cameras?' Holding out his arms, he gestured to the empty room. 'There are no cameras here. There is you, and me—just like there was at the villa on the island.'

Remembering her shock and misery the morning after, she shook her head. 'But you weren't really you. Or maybe you were, and I just thought you were someone else.'

She had been someone else that night too. Someone reckless and uninhibited. And gullible.

His gaze rested intently on her face. 'I don't understand…'

Tears pricked her eyes. 'You don't need to.'

He frowned. 'We're married. I'm your husband.'

Her chest rose and fell as she struggled to breathe. 'I can't believe you can say that with a straight face.' She gazed at him, her heart racing. 'But I suppose it's not surprising you think this is normal. Your whole life is a charade. Why should your marriage be any different?'

Vicè stared at her, a muscle working in his jaw.

'My life was just fine until I married you,' he said slowly.

If she didn't like charades then why was she making him act like some lovesick puppy in public and then relegating him to the sofa when they were alone?

'How is this my fault?' She seemed almost to choke in disbelief.

He stared at her in frustration, her words replaying inside his head. He *didn't* think this was normal. For

him, 'normal' had always been his parents' relationship. Normal, but unattainable.

He was suddenly conscious of his heart hammering
against his ribs.

They had been so happy together, so comfortable,
and yet still sweetly infatuated like the teenagers in love
they had once been. Whereas he—

His body tensed. The idea that he would ever be capable of replicating his parents' marriage had always
seemed too ludicrous to contemplate. So he had done
what he always did—he'd pushed the possibility away,
deliberately choosing a way of life that was the antithesis of theirs.

And his parents had done what they always did too,
indulging him even though he knew that they'd longed
for him to fall in love and settle down.

Remembering his mother's reaction when he'd called
to tell her he was married, he felt his heartbeat slow. It
had been a bittersweet moment. She had been so happy
for him, but also sad that Alessandro hadn't been alive
to see his eldest son finally find love.

What would she say if she knew the truth?

Looking over at Imma, he pushed the thought away,
guilt making his voice harsher than he'd intended. 'This
"charade", as you put it, wasn't my idea.'

She lifted her chin. 'True. But if you'd had your way
I'd have signed over the olive oil company the morning
after we slept together and you and your vile brother
would probably still be toasting your victory in some
bar in Palermo.'

Her description was just about close enough to his
last meeting with Ciro for colour to stain his cheekbones.

Shaking his head, he took a step back, his jaw tightening. 'I don't need this, and I certainly can't live like this for a year.'

'This isn't just about you.'

There was a tautness in her voice, and her mouth was trembling slightly. He realised that she was close to tears.

She sucked in a breath. 'For once I don't want to have to think about what someone else wants or needs. I thought with you—'

As she glanced away he felt his spine stiffen. The events of the last few days must be starting to catch up with her. Or maybe she had been in shock all along.

'You're right. This isn't just about me.' He flattened the anger in his voice, picking his words very carefully, suddenly afraid that the wrong ones would make her run again. 'So tell me what *you* want—what *you* need.'

There was a moment of silence.

'I don't know.' She shook her head. 'I really don't know. I've never known. Maybe if I had none of this would be happening.'

Her shoulders tightened, making her look smaller, wounded, like a bird with a broken wing. Seeing her like that—so diminished, so vulnerable—made him ache inside.

'I doubt that,' he said gently.

He sat down on the sofa, and after a moment, as he'd hoped she would, she sat down beside him.

'There are a lot of reasons why this has happened, *cara*, but you're not one of them.'

She stiffened. 'I know you hate him. My father, I mean. But he's not all bad. He used to be different before…

when my mother was alive. He's just been on his own for too long.'

His pulse stalled. He did hate her father—and yet right now the reason for that hate seemed irrelevant. What mattered more was Imma's pain.

'How old were you when she died?'

'Eight.'

Her stark single-word answer made his heart kick against his ribs. Watching the flicker of sadness in her green eyes, he felt the ache in his chest spread out like a dark rain cloud.

His father's death had felt like something tearing inside him—and he was an adult, a grown man. Imma had had to deal with the loss of her mother as a child.

'He hated not being able to help her,' she said quietly. 'I think that's why he's like he is now. He can't bear the idea of something happening to me and Claudia—something he can't control.'

Vicè felt his stomach clench. In that case he and Ciro had already had their revenge. And just like that his hunger for retribution was gone—diluted and washed away by the tears in her eyes.

'He's your father,' he said. 'Of course he doesn't want to see you hurt.'

It was meant to be a generic response, only for some reason he found himself thinking about his own father. Right up until his death Alessandro had spent his life protecting him, constantly levelling the playing field so that he wouldn't have to compare himself unfavourably to Ciro. In fact, it had been that need to protect his eldest son that had ultimately caused his death.

Something jarred in his chest, as if a depth charge had exploded. He'd made this about Cesare, but it was

actually about him. It had always been about him and
his failings as a son, as a man.

He forced himself to look over and meet her gaze.
'He loves you.'

She nodded slowly. 'But he still misses my mother.
That's why he works so much. Only now he's become
obsessed with building up the business, and...' She hesitated, her face tensing. 'It matters to him—his name, his
legacy. He's never said anything but I know he wishes
he'd had a son. Instead, he's got me. Only I can't ever
be good enough. He wants me to be tough and ruthless,
but he also wants me to be a dutiful daughter. And then
there's Claudia...'

The sudden softness in her eyes cut through him like
a blade. 'You're close?' he asked.

She nodded. 'She was so little when Mamma died.
We had nannies, but they didn't stay long. Papà was so
angry, so exacting. Anyway, she always preferred me.
And I didn't mind. I *wanted* to look after her.'

Her voice sounded scraped and bruised. It made
something hard lodge in his throat. 'You *have* looked
after her.'

'How?' She bit her lip. 'I let her marry Ciro and now
he's broken her heart.' A tear slid down her cheek. 'I
was supposed to take care of her—'

He caught her hands in his. Her whole body was
rigid, braced for disaster. 'You did—you are. But she's
not a child any more, *cara*—'

'You don't understand. I promised Mamma, and now
I've broken that promise.'

She was crying in earnest now and he pulled her onto
his lap, wanting and needing to hold her close, to hold
her for as long as it took to make her feel whole again.

His skin burned with shame as he realised the mistake he'd made. Imma wasn't her father's daughter at all. She was just a little girl who had lost her mother and had to grow up fast. A little girl who had been so busy trying to be a daughter and a mother and a proxy son all at once that she had never had time to be herself. He couldn't bear picturing her little face, her anxious green eyes.

Gently, he stroked her hair. *'Va tutto bene, cara,'* he murmured. 'It's going to be okay. I've got you.'

He understood now how her family had pushed their needs ahead of hers. And he had been no better. In fact, he had been worse. Deliberately and ruthlessly using her as a means to punish her father.

His arms tightened and he kept on smoothing her hair until finally she let out a shuddering breath.

'None of this is your fault, Imma,' he said quietly. 'You're a good sister, and a loyal daughter, but you're way more than the sum of your parts. You're an amazing woman. You're beautiful and sexy and strong and smart. You can be anything you want.' Pulling the towel from around his neck, he gently patted the tears from her cheeks. 'And I'll be there, remember? In the background...'

Her lips curved up, as he had hoped they would.

For a moment they stared at each other in silence.

'You didn't sign up for this,' she said quietly.

'Oh, I signed up for everything, *cara*. Kiss-and-tell interview, miniseries, film franchise...'

He was trying to make her relax, maybe enough to trust him. But he was surprised to find that he was also telling the truth.

Her smile flickered. 'I want to be there for Papà and

Claudia, but I want to be myself too. I thought if I could break free just for one night, lose my virginity to someone I'd chosen, then it would all become clear. Who I am. What I want. And maybe somebody would want me for being me.' She screwed up her face. 'It sounds stupid, saying it out loud.'

He shook his head. 'It's not stupid at all.'

He'd left Sicily to do much the same. Not to lose his virginity, but to put as much distance as possible between himself and his parents' carefully managed disappointment—and, of course, Ciro's effortless success.

'I thought it would be so easy.' Her eyes found his. 'And then I met you.'

'You deserve better,' he said slowly. 'You deserve better than me.' He hesitated. 'How is she? Claudia? Is she okay?'

Her smile faded a little and for a moment he didn't think she was going to reply, but finally she nodded.

'She will be. I'll take of her.'

'I know.' His eyes met hers and he was suddenly conscious of her warm hands on his chest. 'And what about you?'

There was a beat of silence.

'Me?' She seemed stunned by the question. 'I don't— It's not—'

'I want to look after you, Imma.' He stopped. 'Look, I messed up. Ciro too. We were wrong. We made this about you and Claudia and that was wrong,' he repeated. 'Our fight is with your father—not you.' His heart began to beat faster. 'I want to make it up to you. What I'm trying to say is… Could we start this year over?'

Her face didn't change, and nor did she reply.

'If you need more time—' he began.

'I don't,' she said quietly.

He felt a rush of misery and regret, but then his pulse leapt as her hand splayed across his chest.

'But if we start again it has to be different. No more lies, Vicè. No more games. Agreed?'

At that moment, with her body so warm and soft and close to his, he would have agreed to just about anything.

'Agreed,' he said hoarsely.

There was a short silence.

Finally, she cleared her throat. 'You should probably get out of those damp clothes…'

Nodding, he made as though to slide her off his lap, but she didn't move. Instead, her eyes met his.

'Or I could help you…' A little shakily, she ran her fingers down his body to the waistband of his shorts. 'Unless you've changed your mind?'

He stared at her dazedly. *What mind?* Like the rest of him, his mind had melted at the feel of her fingertips on his skin.

A flicker of hope went through him like an electric current and he swallowed, his eyes dropping to her mouth, then lower to the swell of her breasts.

'Is that— Do you— I mean, are you saying what I think you're trying to say?'

His usual effortless eloquence had deserted him. He couldn't remember ever feeling so awkward. But he was shaken by the intensity of his desire, paralysed with fear that he had misunderstood her gesture and words.

'Yes,' she said simply.

It was as if a starter gun had gone off in his head.

Framing her face with his hands, he pulled her closer,

his mouth finding hers, and he felt a shiver running over him as her fingers stroked across his skin.

'I've been thinking about this for days...' he groaned against her mouth.

Shock waves of desire were slamming through his body.

'I've been thinking about it too.'

Her breathing was decidedly unsteady now, and she was pushing him back, back onto the sofa.

'Wait, wait... No—not here. Not on this damn sofa,' he muttered.

It was his last conscious thought as, reaching down, he scooped her up into his arms and carried her upstairs.

As he dropped her gently onto the bed Imma sat up, pulling him closer, her mouth seeking the outline of his arousal through the still damp fabric of his boxer shorts. He grunted, his body jerking forward as her fingers slid over his hip bones and she began to move her lips over the swell of his erection.

His hand caught in her hair. 'Imma...' He swore softly.

Imma felt her stomach clench. Her power to arouse him was shockingly exciting, and he was fiercely aroused. Fingers trembling slightly, she tugged at the waistband of his boxer shorts, heat flaring in her pelvis as she slid them over his hips.

She watched his jaw tighten, the muscles of his arms bunching as she ran her tongue around the blunt, rigid tip, taking it in her mouth. The feel of it jerking and pulsating in her mouth made her head swim.

He groaned, his fingers twisting in her hair, and then he jolted backwards, lifting her face and lowering his mouth to hers, kissing her with a hunger that made liquid heat flood her pelvis.

As her hands reached for him, he batted them away. 'My turn,' he said hoarsely.

His eyes were dark and molten with heat. Pulling her to her feet, he dipped his head, kissed her again, taking his time, running his tongue slowly over her lips then between them, tasting her, slowing her pulse.

She felt his hands on her back and then he was unzipping her dress, sliding it over her body, his hands moving smoothly around to cup her breasts, his thumbs grazing the already swollen tips until she was shaking inside.

And then he was nudging her back onto the bed, his mouth on hers, dropping his head to take first one and then the other nipple into his mouth, rolling his tongue over the tight, ruched skin as her hands clutched his neck and shoulders.

She reached for him again and this time he caught her hands, pinning them to her sides. Deliberately he slid down her body. A shiver of excitement ran through her.

'Let me taste you,' he whispered, and her head fell back, her whole body quivering as he parted her with his tongue.

Her body arched, pressing against his mouth. She had never felt anything like this. She was moaning, shifting restlessly against him, desperately seeking more, her body no longer her own. There was nothing except him…nothing but his warm, firm mouth and the measured, insistent press of his tongue.

Helplessly, she pushed against him, chasing that fluttering, delicate ripple of pleasure, and then her pulse quickened and she felt her body tighten inside, tensing as the ripple became a wave and she cried out, shuddering beneath him.

Releasing her hands, he moved up the bed, licking his way up her body to her mouth. 'I want you, Imma.'

She wrapped her arms around his neck. 'I want you too. Inside me.'

He rolled onto his back, taking her with him so that she was straddling the rigid length of him, hard and hot against the ache between her thighs. Reaching over, he fumbled in a drawer, lifting her gently as he rolled on a condom.

Squirming against him, she moved her hands across his body, over his stomach and down lower, taking him in her hand. He pulled her against him, his fingers tightening around her waist as he lifted her up and pushed into her slowly, easing himself in, inch by inch.

His face was tight with concentration and with the effort of holding back. 'Look at me,' he whispered.

Their eyes met and, gripping her hips, he began to move. She moved with him, and their bodies sought and found a steady, intoxicating rhythm that sent arrows of heat over her skin.

Reaching out, he cupped her breast, squeezing her nipple, and then his hand moved to the swollen bud of her clitoris, caressing her in time to his body's thrusts, his dark eyes never leaving hers.

She rocked against him, feeling the heat rising up inside her again, gripping him with her muscles, holding him as the friction grew. Her skin felt hot and tight. She was hot and tight inside. And suddenly she flexed forward, as though she was trying to climb over him.

He pulled her back, his eyes locking with hers, and

then he pushed up one more time and she felt her body arch as he tensed, his hands clamping around her waist, her gasp of pleasure mingling with his groan.

CHAPTER EIGHT

IT WAS LATE when Vicè woke, the distant sound of a motorboat in the bay dragging him reluctantly from his cocoon of warmth. For a moment he clung on to the last shreds of sleep, and then slowly he opened his eyes and turned his head towards the open French windows.

He had forgotten to draw the curtains, and outside the sky was a marbled swirl of the palest blue and gold, as beautiful as any Renaissance ceiling. But no sky, however beautiful, could compete with the woman lying beside him.

Imma was asleep, her face resting against his shoulder. Her left hand curled loosely on his chest, the other was resting on the pillow, leaving one rosy-tipped breast bared to his gaze.

His heart began to beat faster. With her tousled hair and long dark lashes brushing her cheeks she looked like a painting. There was a softness to her in sleep, a hint of the vulnerability beneath the poise that made him want to pull her close and hold her against him.

He tensed. It was the first time in his life he had felt that way about any woman, and yet even though it was new and unfamiliar he didn't feel panic or confusion. Instead it felt completely natural, like smiling.

But was that so surprising, really?

He might have acted unfairly—ruthlessly, even—but he wasn't a monster, and seeing her cry had horrified him. Naturally he had wanted to comfort her.

His pulse quickened. What had happened next had been completely natural too.

Natural and sublime.

He swallowed, his groin hardening at the memory of how Imma had moved against him. Illuminated in the moonlight, her body had looked like liquid silver—felt like it too.

It had been different from that first time—slower, less frantic, more like riding a wave…an endless, curling wave of pleasure.

But then last time there had been other things in play. Obviously he'd needed to seduce her, but the intensity of his attraction had caught him off guard, made him question his motives so that it had all got tangled up in his head.

Imma had had her own agenda then too. Sleeping with him, losing her virginity, had been her first small act of independence.

Last night, though, it had been far less complicated for both of them.

It had been lust. Pure and simple and irresistible.

There had been no agenda.

He had wanted her and she had wanted him.

Of course they had been fighting it for days—fighting each other for days. But it had been too strong for both of them.

His chest tightened. They had come together as equals and Imma had made him feel things no other woman

had—driven him to a pitch of excitement that had sub-
sumed everything that had happened between them.

Including getting even with her father.

She stirred in his arms and he stared down at her,
replaying that thought, turning it back and forth inside
his head. Yesterday, when she had been so upset, he'd
felt something shift inside him, but he hadn't articulated
it quite so bluntly before. Putting it into words seemed
to make his thoughts move up a gear, give shape to his
feelings.

He felt a rush of relief. Getting even with Cesare
didn't matter any more. His father's business was as
good as his already, and that meant he was free to enjoy
this year with Imma.

Watching her eyelids flutter open, he felt his body
grow even harder.

And he didn't want to waste a second of it.

'Hey,' he said softly.

She stretched her arms, the movement causing the
sheet to fall away from her naked body, sending a jolt
of heat across his already overheated skin. For a moment she stared up at him, her green eyes widening with
confusion, and then she met his gaze.

'Hey...'

Imma stared up at Vicè, her heart pounding. She had
absolutely no idea what to do. Last time she'd been in
the same situation Claudia had called, so she had never
got to this moment of acknowledgement. It had got lost,
swept aside by her sister's revelation. But now there
was nowhere to hide from the truth of what they had
done—what she had done.

Remembering her hoarse, inarticulate cries of pleasure, the way she had pulled his body and then his mouth closer as he'd addressed that relentless ache between her thighs, her cheeks felt suddenly as if they were on fire.

His touch had been electric, every caress sending her closer to the edge, straining for that elusive *something* that would douse the swirling heat at the centre of her body, until finally it had been in her grasp and she had shuddered to stillness in his arms.

She had never felt like that before—not even that first time. It had been beyond anything she'd ever experienced.

As the moonlight had spilled through the windows she had demanded and given pleasure in equal measure, surrendering to the passion he had unleashed. Now, though, in daylight, she felt a little embarrassed.

Understandably.

She had cried all over him, told him things about herself and her life that she had never shared with anyone, and then she'd had sex with him.

Her heart skipped. She'd expected the sex to be incredible—Vice was a generous, gifted lover. But apparently he was also a good listener. Talking to him had been easy—even about things she had held so close and kept secret from others.

'If it's any help, I don't know how to do the morning-after bit either,' he said quietly.

Swallowing, she looked up into his dark eyes. Her whole life she had been a complicated, contained girl, equal parts fear and ambition, always wanting to push back, but too scared to refuse, to demand, to ask.

But she wasn't scared any more.

'What do you usually do?' she asked.

'That's just it.' Leaning over, he stroked her cheek. 'I don't do anything. Spending the night with someone isn't my thing.' His mouth twisted. '*Wasn't* my thing.'

She stared at him uncertainly, trying to ignore the way her stomach was turning over and over in response to the implication of his words.

'But it is now?' she whispered.

A curl of hair had fallen over her breast and, reaching out, he wrapped it around his fingers, drawing her closer so that her mouth was under his.

'Yes, it most definitely is.'

Was that true? Or was he simply saying what she wanted to hear?

There was a moment of silence.

'You don't believe me?' His eyes searched her face.

'I want to…' She hesitated. There was a coldness in her chest, the chill of doubt. 'It's just that before this— you and me—it wasn't real. You had an agenda—'

Vicè hadn't wanted her for herself then. He'd *needed* to seduce her. Only she'd had no idea. So how could she trust her instincts, her senses, now?

'And you think I had one last night?' He grinned. 'What can I say? I had to get off that sofa somehow.' He glanced down, his smile fading. 'I'm joking, *cara*. That wasn't why—' His face stilled. 'Is this about what I said before? About only wanting you to get at your father?'

He stopped, his jaw tightening.

'Look, maybe right at the beginning, at the wedding, it *was* about getting back at him and getting the business back. But when you came out of the bathroom—' He grimaced. 'I promise you I wanted you so badly I wasn't thinking about your father or my father's olive oil company. Actually, I wasn't thinking, full stop.'

Imma bit her lip. She wanted to believe him, but it was hard. Her father and Claudia both needed her. For support, for protection. She had never felt desirable before—just necessary.

His hand covered hers, and the warmth of his fingers thawed the chill in her chest.

He shook his head. '*Lo so, cara.* I know I haven't given you any reason to trust me, but I meant what I said last night. I can't get you out of my head—you're all I've been thinking about.' His mouth twisted. 'Watching you walk downstairs in that dress, those heels... I actually thought I was going to lose control. I was desperate to get to the hotel, so I didn't make a fool of myself.' He gave her the ghost of a smile. 'Although being a fool is what I do best.'

It was the kind of teasing remark that was typical of him, and yet she couldn't help feeling there was something beneath the banter.

She stared into his eyes. 'You're not a fool.'

'I'm a fool for you,' he said lightly.

She smiled at that and, lifting his hand, he stroked her hair away from her face. 'You know, I think I'm getting pretty good at this morning-after bit,' he murmured.

'Is that right?' Her lips curved upward, caught in the honeyed trap of his gleaming dark eyes and teasing smile.

'Yeah...'

Their eyes met, and then his mouth dropped, and then he kissed her. She felt something stir inside—a flickering heat that made her body ripple to life and tighten in response.

Tipping his head back, he stared down at her, and

then he ran a finger slowly along the line of her collarbone. 'Although I might just need a little bit more practice…'

His voice was warm with desire, and she felt an answering warmth start to spread over her skin as he took her face between his hands and bent his head to kiss her again.

She wanted him, and she was willing to act on that want. She was making a choice and she was choosing Vicè.

It was a feather-light kiss. But then his mouth fused with hers and she whimpered softly as he moved his tensile muscular body over her.

Gripping his hips, she stretched out beneath him. He entered her slowly, giving her time to adjust, inching forward in time with her soft sighs of pleasure. But she needed him *now*—all of him—and she arched upward, pressing herself against the smooth, polished heat of his skin, wrapping her legs around his hips.

She was already aroused, and soon she was growing dizzy, intoxicated by the hard, steady rhythm of his body. A moan of pleasure climbed in her throat, and then a fierce heat blossomed inside her as her muscles tightened around him and she let go in time to his thrust of release.

Later—much later—they sat outside beneath the canopy of wisteria, enjoying a late brunch on the terrace.

'What are you thinking?' Vicè asked.

Turning, Imma smiled. He was staring at her across the table, his dark eyes fixed on her face.

Her pulse skipped. The shock of his beauty never seemed to fade. Any other man would have been eclipsed by the decadent glamour of the Dolce, but in his cream linen trousers, short-sleeved shirt and loafers, he looked like a poster playboy for the Italian Riviera.

With effort, she pulled her gaze away to the view past his shoulder, where huge white yachts floated serenely on an aquamarine sea. 'I was thinking how lucky you are.'

He raised an eyebrow. 'That's crazy—so was I.'

Smiling, she glanced past him at the panorama below. 'You have such a beautiful view here.'

'No, that's not what's beautiful here,' he said softly.

She shook her head. 'Do you ever stop?'

'You made me, remember?' He rolled his eyes. 'You said we had to eat food. Or get dressed or something...'

Their eyes met. She and Vicè had taken a shower together. Her cheeks felt suddenly warm. At first they had just washed one another, but then the soap had got dropped, and then he had shown her other, more inventive and thrilling ways to pass the time beneath the warm, tumbling spray.

'Somebody was knocking at the door. You were naked.'

'It was Matteo,' he protested. 'And he's seen me naked hundreds of times...' He paused. 'You know, at the orgies.'

Her mouth dropped open. 'The orgies—'

'At the hotel. Surely you've read about them?'

He was grinning.

'Oh, very funny, Vicè.'

He got up, moving smoothly around the table to grab her, laughing softly when she tried to bat him away.

'*Cara*, come on. I'm sorry. I couldn't help it. You just look so sexy when you're outraged.'

'I wasn't outraged. I was—'

'Jealous?'

His dark eyes were watching her intently and she felt her pulse jump.

She lifted her chin. 'Curious.'

'Well, you're going to have to stay curious, I'm afraid,' he said softly, and his calm tone was at odds with the slight tightening of his jaw. 'You're mine, and I'm not about to share you with anyone.'

Leaning forward, he kissed her fiercely, parting her lips to deepen the kiss until her head was spinning.

'Vicè…' Closing her eyes, she whispered his name, her voice trembling, her stomach flipping over in frantic response to his words as much as to his mouth, her body screaming in protest as slowly he released her.

Opening her eyes, she found him still watching her, his face impassive again.

'So,' he said. 'How would you like to spend the rest of the day?'

He shifted against her, and as his arm grazed her shoulder blade her heart jerked. Earlier, she'd been worried this wasn't real. Now, though, she could see that a far more likely scenario was her letting it get real in her imagination. Getting ahead of herself, making connections that simply weren't there and never would be.

For her, every soft word and dark glance might feel meaningful, but the truth was Vicè liked to flirt. It was his default setting. He liked sex too, and it was great that sex had unlocked this wild, uninhibited woman hiding inside of her. But the year was supposed to be about discovering who she was, and sex was only a part of that.

Essentially, the facts hadn't changed. Theirs was a marriage of convenience and in a year it would be over.

She needed to remember that. And until it was over she was going to have to set some rules.

First rule: take a step back. Stop allowing the passion she found in his arms to mislead her and make her forget why she had agreed to this marriage in the first place.

Second rule: get out there and do and try everything at least once. How else was she going to work out who she was?

Smoothing her sundress over her knees, she said offhandedly, 'I know I said I didn't want the two of us to go out in public again, but I'd really like to take a proper look around.'

If he noticed the forced casualness in her voice he didn't acknowledge it. Instead he leaned back in his seat and gave her an approving smile. 'Of course, *cara*. It would be my pleasure.'

Imma found the hours that followed both enjoyable and enlightening.

The hotel was larger than she had realised, but still small enough to feel like a private sanctuary, with a decor that cleverly blurred the lines between vintage and contemporary, homely and hip. Chequerboard floors sat alongside huge gilt mirrors and faded hand-painted frescoes of the Dolce's guests and staff.

'My friend Roberto painted them in exchange for my letting him have a room over the winter,' Vicè explained as they wandered out into the lushly beautiful tiered gardens.

There were grander, more opulent, more glamorous hotels, she was sure. But there was something special about the Dolce.

She glanced over at where Vicè stood, joking with

Edoardo, the hotel's legendary seventy-year-old pianist, who played everything from show tunes to swing for the guests sipping *aperitivi* on the terrace.

Unlike most hotels, everything felt authentic, rather than staged to create a certain vibe. But then not many hotels so closely embodied the personality of their owner. The Dolce *was* Vicè, and so, like him, it was effortlessly glamorous, flirty and cool.

'Do you want to dance?'

Vicè had stopped in front of her.

'Edo can play anything. Although I'd steer clear of rap or thrash metal.'

Biting into her smile, she shook her head, feeling suddenly conspicuous as around them everyone seemed to sit up straighter and glance covertly in their direction.

'Maybe later.'

Grinning, he took her hand. 'I'll hold you to that. Come on, I want to show you my favourite view. *Ciao*, Edo.' He turned and waved at the older masn.

'*Ciao*, boss. Maybe catch up with you and Signora Trapani later? At the party!'

Imma frowned. 'There's a party?'

'Not here—on the yacht.' When Imma raised her eyebrows, he shrugged. 'I have a yacht—the *Dolphin*. I keep her down in the bay for guests who like to cut loose. There's a party on board tonight, but obviously I wasn't going to go.'

She felt a ripple of relief—and then, remembering her refusal to dance, she stiffened her shoulders. What had happened to rule number two?

'Why not?' she said quickly. 'I'd like to go.'

'You would? Okay…well, if that's what you want

to do, great.' He shook his head. 'You are full of surprises, *cara*.'

She gave him a quick, tight smile. Full of fear, more like. How did you even 'cut loose'?

'You're very quiet,' he said a moment later, as he led her along a shady path. 'If you've changed your mind about the party——'

'I haven't.' She stared up at him. 'I was just thinking that you're full of surprises too.'

He eyed her sideways. 'Then you're in a minority of one. Most people think they can read me like a book.' His eyes met hers. 'At a guess, I'd say a well-thumbed easy read—a beach blockbuster, maybe.'

He was smiling, but she had that same feeling she'd had before—that there was something more than what he was saying. And suddenly there was nothing she wanted to know more than what he'd left unsaid.

'That's what you *let* them think.'

He'd let her think that too, at first. Now, though, she could see that there was more to him —a whole lot more.

Take the Dolce. She might have limited hands-on business experience, but she understood enough to know that running one required more than charm and a sexy smile.

His guests loved him. His staff too. She could sense real affection and admiration, and they worked hard for him. He seemed to bring out the best in people. Or at least reveal their untapped potential.

'You have a gift, Vicè,' she said slowly. 'You've made this like a wonderful private club that's open to everyone. And you did it on your own.'

He shrugged. 'It's a living. It's not exactly in Ciro's league. He's Mr Midas.'

They had reached the villa now and, frowning, she followed him upstairs. 'Maybe. But some things are more important than money—and I know you believe that or we wouldn't both be here.'

It felt strange, putting it that way, but it was true. Vicè cared about his father's legacy enough to put aside his distaste and marry the daughter of his enemy. He had wanted revenge on her father, but he had also thrown her a lifeline by agreeing to marry her for a year.

And if revenge was all he was after he certainly wouldn't have agreed to sleep on any sofa.

'You care about your staff, your guests, your family. And it shows. You should be proud of that—of everything you've achieved. I'm sure your family is.'

'Careful, *cara*. I'm already "impossibly arrogant".'

She recognised her own words, but she didn't smile. 'Actually, I don't think you are,' she said quietly.

His eyes locked with hers.

'You're very smart, Imma.' Lifting a hand, he stroked her dark hair away from her face. 'Way too smart for me.'

Her heart began to beat faster and she felt heat break out on her skin. Vicè was wrong. If she was smart she would follow her own rules and stop her body reacting to his lightest touch.

'Not always.' Glancing round the bedroom, she frowned. 'I thought you were going to show me your favourite view?'

'I'm looking at it,' he said softly. He hesitated, his eyes never leaving her face. Then, 'Although I might need to make one small adjustment...'

He took a step towards her and, hooking the thin straps of her dress with his thumbs, he slipped them down over her shoulders. A muscle flickered in his jaw as it slid down her body, pooling around her feet.

Her mouth dried. Caught in the beam of his dark, shimmering gaze, she felt herself melt.

'Perfect,' he said hoarsely.

He leaned over to kiss the bare skin of her throat, and then she was pulling him backwards, onto the bed, all rules forgotten and broken.

'I hope you don't mind, but I bought you something for tonight.'

Leaning forward, Vicè planted a kiss on Imma's lips. As she stared up at him dazedly he sat down on the bed, handing her a large cardboard box wrapped in ribbon.

'I'm going to go and get changed, and then I've got a couple of things to go over with Matteo. Come down when you're ready.'

Ten minutes later he was downstairs, pouring himself and Matteo a glass of wine, his eyes dutifully scanning the guest list.

But his mind was elsewhere.

After they had made love Imma had fallen asleep, but he had been too restless to doze off. Lying next to her soft, naked body had been impossible too, so he'd got dressed and wandered down to the town for the early-evening *passeggiata*.

He'd been wandering through the square, past the cafes and bars, stopping occasionally to greet people, when he'd seen it.

It was the first dress, the first anything, he'd ever bought for a woman.

His mother didn't count.

He hadn't blinked—just walked in through the door

of the boutique and walked out again five minutes later, with the box under his arm and a stupid grin on his face.

It was only now that he was wondering why he'd felt the need to get her a gift. Why he was suddenly so keyed up, so desperate to see her happy.

But wasn't it obvious?

She'd been upset, in tears, and he'd felt guilty. *Great.* He could add it to the teetering pile of guilt he already carried around.

His breath scraped his throat as he remembered their conversation.

Imma thought he was an amazing businessman. A self-made man. The pride of his family. *What a joke.* She'd been closer to the mark when she'd accused him of living a charade.

His whole life was a charade. And the worst part was that his father—the one person who had known his weaknesses, his flaws—had lost his life playing along with it.

He wanted to tell her the truth, but he couldn't bear the idea of losing the respect and trust he'd gained. So now he was trapped in yet another charade.

Only how long would it be before he messed up and she saw him for what he really was? It was only a matter of when, and how, and in the meantime there was nothing he could do but wait for things to fall apart.

'Any problems, boss?'

Glancing at Matteo, he shook his head. He'd barely looked at the names on the guest list, but frankly he didn't care who was going to the party as long as Imma was there.

His stomach knotted.

He wanted to show her that he wasn't just a playboy who used his hotel as a private clubhouse. Okay, it was true that if Ciro had been running the business he would have already turned it into a global chain of luxury hotels. But his business was about more than world domination.

It was about people. Treating people like VIPs. And tonight he wanted to make Imma feel special.

He wanted her to enjoy herself. To relax, to laugh, to smile. More specifically, he wanted her to turn that sweet, shy smile his way.

'It all looks great, Matteo.'

The two men stood up and Vicè clapped his manager on the shoulder.

Matteo grinned. 'Okay, *capo*. I'll catch up with y—' He stopped midsentence, his mouth hanging open.

Turning, Vicè did the same. Imma was hovering in the doorway, biting her lip. Her hair was in some kind of chignon, and with her smoky eye make-up and glossy lips she looked as if she'd wandered off the set of a Fellini film.

And then there was her dress.

Beside him, Matteo whistled softly. 'I'll leave you to it, boss.'

He skirted past Imma, smiling, and Vicè heard the soft click of the door.

She turned, the smile she had given Matteo still on her face. 'Could you finish zipping me up, please?'

'Of course.' Finding his voice, he crossed the room. 'There—done.'

He couldn't stop himself from dropping a kiss to the column of her throat, his body hardening as he felt her shiver of response.

'Thank you for the dress,' she murmured.

'You look beautiful.'

Glancing down, he swallowed. The heavy satin looked like freshly poured cream, and his groin clenched as his brain feverishly rushed to bring that image to life in glorious 3D Technicolor.

'It fits perfectly.'

She smiled. 'You look pretty perfect too.' Her eyes skimmed appreciatively over his dark suit.

Recovering his poise, he made a mocking bow. 'This old thing?' As she started to laugh he held out his arm. 'Shall we go?'

Gazing across the water, Vicè breathed in the fresh, salt-tinged air.

The blunt outline of the motorboat was skimming easily over the indigo waves, the hum of its engine lost in the vastness of the bay. Behind him the glittering bracelet of lights along the Portofino seafront was starting to fade.

He glanced over to where Imma sat beside him. Her green eyes were wide with nerves or excitement or both, her cheeks flushed already from the rushing breeze.

They were on their way to the yacht, and he was still slightly surprised at her eagerness to go. But then nothing should surprise him about this woman who had agreed to be his wife. She had been surprising him ever since she'd walked into that church and refused to meet his eye.

Leaning back against his seat, he studied her profile.

Immacolata Buscetta. Prized eldest daughter of a notorious bully and a thief and a chip off the old block. But Imma was most definitely not what she seemed. The clues had been there. He'd just been too blinkered with anger to do anything more than focus on the obvious.

He had believed what he'd wanted to believe, and the fact that she was not the woman he had thought her to be was unsettling enough. More unsettling still was the fact that had she just walked away he would never have known his mistake.

Never got to know her.

The thought of that happening made his stomach clench.

Or maybe it was the sudden swell of the sea as the motorboat slowed alongside the yacht.

'Party's started,' he remarked as they stepped on board.

He felt a rush of exhilaration beat through his body in time to the music drifting down through the warm evening air. Here, he was king. This was his world. And he loved it. He loved the laughter, the pulsing bass notes and the waiters with their trays of champagne. He loved the buzz of energy and the beautiful women with their sequins and high heels.

His eyes roamed slowly down over Imma's body. Actually, make that one specific woman…

His heartbeat stalled. But who said anything about love?

Turning towards her, he caught her hand and pulled her towards him. 'Let's join in.'

Imma felt her heart start to pound.

As they made their way through the crowded yacht she felt even more exposed than when they'd first walked into the hotel together.

Everyone was so beautiful. Particularly the women.

All of whom were looking at Vicè with naked longing. She knew what they were thinking. It would be like seeing a peahen with her mate. They must all be wondering how such an ordinary bird could attract this glittering peacock.

'It's okay,' she said quietly as someone called out Vicè's name. 'I think everyone here believes we're married. You don't need to stay glued to my side all evening.'

His brows locked together. 'I couldn't care less what they believe, *cara*. I'm staying glued to your side because I want to. I like being with you, okay?'

She stared at him, her doubts suddenly losing shape, growing hazy next to his muscular solidity and the steady focus of his dark eyes.

'Okay then…'

It took them some time to actually get anywhere. People kept coming over to talk to him, and every person needed introducing.

'Do you know *everyone* here?' she asked as finally they made their way out into the deck, what seemed like several hours later.

'I suppose I do.'

Glancing back into the crowded saloon, he made a face. 'I know that must seem crazy, but it's what I do—it's who I am.'

She smiled. 'You have a lot of friends.'

And yet he still seemed to prefer her. The thought made warm bubbles of happiness rise inside her.

He smiled down at her. 'They're your friends too now. Now, how about that dance?'

'You took the words right out of my mouth.'

Swinging round, Vicè grinned at the lanky dark-haired man standing beside him. 'Is that the best you've got, Roberto? Really?'

'I'm a starving artist. I'm used to humbling myself.'

'You're an artist?' Imma frowned. 'Are you the Roberto who painted those frescoes in the hotel?'

'One and the same.' He made a small bow. 'But I would much prefer to paint you, *bella*.'

Groaning, Vicè slipped his arm around Imma's waist. 'Get your own wife and paint her.'

'This is your *wife*?' The other man raised an eyebrow appreciatively. 'Lucky man.'

'Yes, I am,' he agreed.

Imma felt a blush suffuse her cheeks as he stared down into her eyes.

'Very lucky...'

Roberto shook his head. 'I think I need to come up with a reason to get you alone, Signora Trapani. Then I can give you the low-down on this guy.'

'She already knows.' Vicè shook his head. 'Now, go and stretch some canvases, or whatever it is you do when you're not bugging me.'

Imma glanced up at him. 'Are you okay?'

'Of course.' He smiled. 'I just want to dance with my wife.'

She looked so beautiful. A little nervous but she was hiding it well, so that only he would have known. His spine tensed. He liked knowing that he could see beneath her poise, but it made him feel responsible.

Only how could he be responsible for Imma? He could barely manage his own life, let alone someone else's.

Taking her hand, he drew her away from the dance floor.

She frowned. 'I thought you wanted to dance.'

'I do. But I want it to be just the two of us.'

He thought back to when she'd said he had a lot of friends. Were they friends? He stared at the faces, feeling suddenly confused. Tonight none of them seemed even the slightest bit familiar. Nor did he feel like talking to any of them.

Normally he liked being at the centre of the crowd, surrounded by happy, smiling faces. But tonight the music was too loud, the lights too bright.

Turning, he led her through a door marked *Private*, up a spiral staircase and back outside.

'That's better,' he said softly. 'I can hear myself think.'

'You need to *think*? What kind of dancing are you planning?' she teased.

He smiled and pulled her closer. He thought about the party downstairs. And then she leaned forward, her cheek pressing into his shoulder, and he forgot about everything but the feel of her body against his and his hunger for her.

He cleared his throat. 'Are you having fun?'

Looking up at him, she nodded. 'Yes, but I'm happy to leave whenever you are.'

Her lips were parted and her eyes looked dark in the moonlight. Without replying, he took her hand and led her back downstairs, his self-control unravelling with every step and turn.

CHAPTER NINE

RAISING A HAND to shield her eyes from the sun, Imma put down her book and gazed across the terrace. It really was very hot today—far too hot to read anyway.

Totti, Matteo's French bulldog, lay panting beneath the wilting shrubs, and down in the bay even the motorboats were still, smothered into silence by the heat haze shimmering above the blue water.

She was lying on a lounger, half shielded from the sun by the trailing wisteria that overhung the terrace. And for the first time since arriving in Portofino she was alone in the villa.

Vicè was dealing with something at the hotel—she wasn't sure what. After a night of making love she had been too sleepy to do more than mumble when he'd said goodbye.

At first she'd been glad to have a few moments to herself. To think back to last night...to how he'd held her close as if she was precious to him. She knew he had held her because he liked her, and in his arms all those years of wondering who she was had dissolved.

But, much as she might have liked to daydream about those blissful hours when he had chosen her over everyone else, she was still Claudia's big sister and after a few days of just texting she needed to check in with her properly.

Feeling guilty, she had called her, expecting her to be tearful and crushed and needing reassurance.

She had been wrong on all counts.

Claudia had been quiet, but calm, and instead of wanting to talk she had been the one to end their conversation.

Imma shifted against the cushions. Of course she was glad that her sister was coping so well, and yet it was a shock. Claudia had always been so sweet and shy. But she had sounded focused, determined—like a different person, in fact.

'There you are.'

She jumped slightly as a cool hand slid over her shoulder and a shadow blocked the sun. Dropping down onto the lounger beside her, Vicè leaned over and kissed her softly on the mouth.

Her heart bumped against her ribs and she tensed, her breath hitching in her throat, her body taut and aching. Surely she should be used to his touch by now? But she was already melting on the inside, her limbs and her stomach dissolving into a puddle of need.

For a moment her lips clung to his, and she was lost in the warmth and the dizziness of his kiss, and then she shifted back, blinking into the light as he lifted his mouth from hers.

'Was it okay?' she asked quickly. 'At the hotel?'

'It's fine. The guests in Room Sixteen decided to record some new songs. At three a.m. Then they got upset when someone uploaded them to the web.' He grinned. 'Here—I thought you might need a drink. I know I do.'

Squinting into the sun, he handed her a glass. 'One perfect Negroni.'

She raised an eyebrow. 'At ten o'clock?'

'It's pretty perfect at any time.' The ice clinked as he tipped his glass up to his mouth. 'Come on, *cara*, this is supposed to be your year of living dangerously.'

As she took the drink, he glanced up at the flawless sky.

'*Accidenti*, it's hot today! If you want we can take the yacht out later. It'll be cooler at sea. We could head down the coast to the Bay of Poets.'

With his shirt hanging loosely open and his dark hair flopping into his eyes he *looked* like a poet, she thought. She felt her stomach clench. He might not be as bad or as mad as Lord Byron, but he was certainly dangerous to know.

Dangerous to her self-control.

'Does that mean you're going to write me a poem?'

His eyes gleamed. 'I might. What rhymes with Immacolata?'

She smiled. 'Poetry doesn't have to rhyme. Free verse doesn't follow any rules.'

'That sounds more like it.'

His dark eyes rested on her face, the corners of his mouth curving up into a smile that was so unapologetically flirtatious that she burst out laughing.

'You're impossible.'

'So I'm told.' He frowned. 'You're not getting too hot in the sun, are you?'

She felt her pulse accelerate, and a shivery pleasure danced down her spine as he leaned forward and ran his fingers lightly over her stomach, stopping at the triangle of her bright yellow bikini bottom.

'Maybe I should rub in some oil,' he said softly. 'Just to be on the safe side…'

That might work for her skin, she thought, but no amount of oil was going to appease the heat inside her.

She lifted her chin. 'Or I could just go for a swim.'

He grinned. 'Chicken.'

Ignoring his teasing gaze, she stood up and walked down the steps into the pool. He watched her as she did a slow length, and then, downing his drink, he stripped off his shirt and dived in, slicing through the water without a ripple and surfacing beside her.

His hands circled her waist.

'You don't need to hold me.' She held his gaze. 'I can swim.'

'That's not why I'm holding you.'

He pulled her closer and her eyes widened with shock as she felt the thickness of his erection through his shorts.

'If I pass out, I'm relying on you to get me to safety.'

His voice had a huskiness to it that made her heart thump out of time.

'So you see me as some kind of lifebelt?'

His eyes dropped to her mouth, then lower to where the water was lapping at her breasts. 'If that means you're going to wrap yourself around my waist, then yes.'

'I think it's you that needs cooling off, Vicenzu,' she teased. And, grabbing hold of his head, she pushed him under the water, then turned and swam away.

He came up, spluttering, and swam after her, snatching for her ankles and making her scream with laughter and terror until finally he caught her in the shallow end.

Laughing down at her, he scooped her into his arms

and carried her out of the pool, his dark eyes glittering. 'You are going to pay for that, Signora Trapani. With interest.'

Her hands gripped his bicep as he lowered his mouth to hers...

'What the—' He swore softly, his face creasing with irritation. On the other side of the terrace his phone was ringing. 'I won't answer it.'

'It's fine. Honestly.' Her body twitched in protest but she managed to smile. 'It might be important.'

Grimacing, he put her down and strode over to his phone. Picking it up, he glanced briefly at the screen, and her throat tightened as he immediately turned away to answer it.

It was Ciro. It must be. There was a tension to his body that hadn't been there before and he clearly didn't want her to hear his conversation.

Moments earlier she had been laughing in his warm arms. Now, though, she felt as if someone had slapped her in the face. For the last few days she had all but forgotten how he and Ciro had plotted together against her family. Now here was a blunt reminder.

Her body stiffening with misery, she watched him pace back and forth, his head bent over the phone, and then, picking up her book, she walked quickly back into the villa.

Inside it was dark and cool and she felt some of her panic recede.

Nothing had changed.

So why did she feel as if it had?

'Imma?'

She turned. Vicè was standing behind her, a frown still touching his handsome face.

'I'm sorry, but I won't be able to take you down the coast today.' His eyes avoided hers. 'Something's come up—'

'What's he done now?' Her heart was suddenly thumping so hard she could hardly speak. Claudia had sounded fine earlier, but—

'Who?' He stared at her uncomprehendingly.

'Your brother.'

'Ciro?' His eyes widened. 'I don't know. I wasn't talking to him. That was my mother.'

Her pulse slowed. She saw that his face had none of its usual animation, and something in the set of his shoulders made her hold her breath.

'Is she okay?'

Vicè had told her very little about his mother. All she knew was that Audenzia had moved to Florence, to live with her sister and brother-in-law.

He shook his head. 'She's had a fall.'

'Oh, Vicè…' Reaching out, she touched his hand. 'I'm sorry.'

'She's okay—just a bit shaken up. She's not alone. My aunt and uncle are with her. But—'

'She wants you.' She finished his sentence. 'Of course she does. We can leave right now. I'll go and get changed.'

'You want to come with me?' He looked confused.

'Of course. You can't go all that way on your own.' Now it was her turn to look confused. 'And besides, won't it look odd if I don't go with you?'

He didn't reply and she stared at him, suddenly mortified. Earlier, in bed and when they'd been laughing by the pool, she had been lulled into forgetting that this was just a mutually convenient arrangement.

But clearly Vicè hadn't forgotten. For him, this was still about sun and sex and drinking cocktails by the pool. It was obvious—*should have been obvious to her*—that his mother would be off limits. He didn't need or want her there for reasons that were glaringly self-evident.

She felt his fingers tighten around hers.

'I'm sorry,' he said slowly. 'I'd love you to come with me. It just didn't occur to me that you'd want to.'

'No, *I'm* sorry.' She tried to smile. 'I mean, why would you want me there? After everything my father's done?'

'I don't care about what your father did.' A muscle flickered in his jaw and he pulled her closer. 'Look at me, Imma. I don't care—not any more. I told you that's over. Done. Finished. Forgotten. I just didn't want you to have to lie to my mother that's all, to pretend that you love me—'

Her arms tightened around him. 'This isn't about me. It's about your mother. So if you want me to be there, I'll be there.'

Tipping her face up to his, he kissed her softly. 'I'd like that very much.'

They were about an hour away from Florence when steam began swirling up from the bonnet of the car. Swearing softly, Vicè pulled off the road and switched off the engine.

'What's the matter?'

'It's overheated. Wait here. I'm going to flip the bonnet and check the radiator.'

Imma leaned back in her seat. Without the air-conditioning the car began to grow warmer immediately, and she was opening the window when he returned.

'Sorry about this. It'll be fine. We just need to wait about half an hour for it to cool down a little, and then I can add some water. It gets a bit moody when it's hot.' He gave her a wry smile. 'Which you'd probably worked out already.'

'Actually, I don't know anything about cars,' she admitted. 'I can't even drive.'

'What?' He was staring at her in disbelief. 'Why not?'

She felt her cheeks grow warm. 'There was no point. Papà wouldn't have liked me going out on my own, and anyway I have a driver.'

Her heart began to thump. Why had she mentioned her father? The confusion between them back at the villa seemed to be forgotten, but reminding him why his mother was now alone had been stupid and insensitive.

But after the briefest hesitation his eyes met hers. 'I'll teach you to drive, if you want. Maybe not in this one—like I say, she's a bit moody. But I've got other cars.'

'You'd do that?'

'Of course. A year's plenty long enough.'

She kept on smiling, but the implicit reminder that this was a temporary arrangement stung a little more than she knew it should. Not liking the way that made her feel, she searched her mind for something neutral to say.

'So why did you drive this car today if it's so moody?'

His face stilled. 'My mother likes to see me using it. It was my father's car. His pride and joy. We used to work on it together when I was a teenager.'

She felt her stomach knot. He seemed distracted by the memory—wistful, even.

'I bet he loved spending man-time with you and Ciro.'

He hesitated. 'Ciro wasn't there. He couldn't see the point in wasting half a day getting covered in oil. It was just me and Papà.'

The ache in his voice made that knot tighten.

'You must miss him so much.'

This time there was a definite pause before he answered. 'Every day.' His mouth tensed. 'I'm sorry you didn't get to meet him. You would have liked him and he would have liked you.'

'I wish I'd met him,' she said truthfully. 'From everything I've heard he was a true gentleman and a good man.'

Alessandro Trapani's reputation was, in fact, the antithesis of her father's

Vicè smiled, but the expression in his eyes was bleak. 'He *was* a good man. He had no failings, no flaws.' His mouth twisted. 'Actually, that's not true.'

He glanced away, and now the knot in her stomach was making her feel sick.

'He had one major flaw. Me.'

She stared at him in silence, shocked and distressed by the pinched lines around his eyes as much as the brutality of his statement.

'I don't think that's true,' she said slowly.

'Yeah, you do.' A muscle pulled at his jaw. 'You saw right through me.'

Slowly, she shook her head. 'If that were true then I would never have slept with you.'

'Oh, you would still have slept with me, *cara*. You

would have told yourself that I needed saving, or maybe that I was misunderstood,' he said calmly. 'That's what you do, Imma. You take care of people…you protect them.'

'And so do you. You take care of people. That's why they like you.'

Now he shook his head. 'They like me because of how I look and how I make them feel about themselves.'

'Your father didn't feel that way.'

'No, he didn't. My father knew everything about me. He saw my weaknesses and he loved me anyway. He loved me completely and unconditionally and that was his weakness—like I said, I was his flaw.'

He smiled at her crookedly.

'You asked me why he didn't come to me and Ciro for help. Do you remember? You said that neither of his sons had what was needed to save him.'

'I was angry.'

'But you were right. Almost right.' His shoulders tensed. 'He couldn't come to me. He knew I didn't have any money because I'd just asked him for a loan. Another loan.'

The tension was spilling over into his shoulders now. And his spine was so taut it looked as though it might snap.

'He could have gone to Ciro. But he didn't. He wouldn't—he didn't want to do that *to me*. And that's why he's dead. Because he wanted to protect me—my ego, my pride. Just like he did my entire life.'

Imma felt sick. 'That's not true, Vicè.'

'It *is* true.' His voice cracked. 'You were right about me. My whole life is a charade and my father played along with it until it killed him. And, you know, the worst part is that since his death I've had to just get on with it—and I have. So I could have done it all along. I could have been the son he wanted…the son he needed. Maybe if I had he'd still be alive.'

Tears pricked the back of her eyes. The pain in his voice cut her like a razor.

Reaching out, she took his hand. 'You *were* the son he wanted. The son he loved. And if he protected you then it's because he was your father and that was his job,' she said, her longing to ease his pain giving emphasis to her words. 'And I don't think that's why he didn't ask you for help. With his reputation he could have gone to any number of people. But good men have their pride too.'

His fingers squeezed hers. 'You're a wonderful person, Imma. And I hate how I've hurt you.'

'That's done. Finished. Forgotten.' Lifting her hand, she stroked his cheek. 'You've forgiven my father and I've forgiven you.'

'I don't deserve to be forgiven. I should have made Ciro wait. Let his anger cool. Then probably none of this would have happened. But I felt guilty—guilty that we'd lost our father because of me.' His face creased. 'And then I messed it up anyway.'

Imma shook her head. 'You didn't mess it up. *He* did. Claudia heard him leaving you a message. I checked your phone afterwards, just to be certain. It was Ciro who messed up. Not you.'

Vicè stared at her in confusion.

Ciro had messed up? He almost wanted to laugh.

But then he caught sight of Imma's face. Her green

eyes were wide and worried, and—his heartbeat stalled—she was worried about *him*.

'It doesn't change anything.' His chest felt tight. 'It's still on me, Imma. I was ashamed and angry with *myself*. But it was easier to blame your father, and that's why I went along with everything. And now I've hurt you, and you're having to live my charade too.'

'Okay. But if you're to blame, then so is Ciro,' she said firmly. 'And your father. And my father. They're all responsible for their actions.' She frowned. 'And so am I. I'm not just a victim, and you're not the villain.'

Her eyes met his, and he felt something inside him loosen.

'Everyone is a work in progress, Vicè. Every new day is a chance to start again and do better. And it's being with you that's taught me that. Maybe you need to accept that too, and let go of the past?'

He stared at her, her words replaying inside his head, the rhythm of her voice soothing him. For the first time since his father's death, maybe even before, he felt calm. The heaviness inside him that he hid so well was lifting.

She was right. Before, everything had always seemed so fixed, so definite—his failings, his relationship with his father and Ciro—so that for years he'd just been blindly following the script. But already he knew that he had changed, and was still changing.

Leaning forward, he tilted her face up to his and kissed her softly. 'I've never met anyone like you, Imma. You're a remarkable woman, and I am so very sorry for how I hurt you.'

Her eyes were bright. 'I know. But I meant what I said. I really have forgiven you.' She hesitated, her fingers trembling against his arms. 'And that's why I want you to have the business *now*. I don't want to wait a year. When we get back to the villa I'll sign it over to you.'

He stared at her in stunned silence. It was the reason he had married her. He had turned his life upside down to pursue this very moment. Only now that it was here he realised he no longer cared about it.

'I don't want it.'

As the words left his mouth his body loosened, his shoulders lifted free of some invisible burden. Ciro could rage all he liked. He was done with revenge.

Now it was her turn to stare. 'I don't understand.'

He pulled her closer. 'Getting even was never really my thing, *cara*. And anyway, I'm too good-looking to be the bad guy.'

Watching her mouth curve into a smile, he felt a rush of relief. He'd hurt her, and he couldn't change the past. But if he let her keep the business then he could at least look her in the eye.

Only what did that mean for their 'arrangement'?

His pulse slowed. Theoretically, there was no reason for them to stay married. Or rather for him to stay married. But the thought of not waking up next to her made something tighten in his chest for one very obvious reason.

He hadn't finished with her, and he knew from the pulse beating in her throat that she felt the same way.

His eyes locked with hers. 'But I still want you to have this year. Actually, I want us both to have this year. We can work on ourselves.' He smiled. 'Or, better still, each other.'

And at the end of the year she would leave and, having had his fill, he would go back to the life he loved. That, after all, was what he wanted—wasn't it?

Reaching into the back seat, he grabbed a bottle of water.

'I'm going to top up the radiator—and then I think we should probably go and see my mother.'

Following his uncle Carlo through the beautiful fifteenth-century apartment, Vicè felt his heartbeat speed up. Carlo had reassured him that Audenzia was doing well, but after what had happened with his father he wanted to see her with his own eyes.

'This way.'

Carlo pulled open a door, stepping aside as a uniformed maid scurried past, blushing as she caught sight of Vicè.

'They're in the salon, and I should warn you that emotions are running high,' he said dryly to Imma. 'They both dote on Vicè—'

Vicè grinned. 'Understandably…'

'Inexplicably was the word I was seeking.' Carlo winked at Imma. 'But when you walk in the room, *mia cara*, I fear that things could get quite out of hand.'

'It's what always happens to me,' Vicè said softly, pretending to wince as Imma punched him on the arm.

He glanced sideways into her beautiful face. He still couldn't quite believe he'd had that conversation with her in the car. He had never talked about his relationship with his father to anyone. Never admitted his worst fears. Not even to Ciro or his mother.

Especially not to Ciro or his mother.

But talking to Imma had been so easy. She had listened and she hadn't judged. She had talked gently and calmly, almost as if he'd been in some kind of accident.

He certainly felt as if he'd been in one—except there

were no physical injuries…just the pain of grief and the ache of loss.

But now he felt lighter. She had helped reconcile the past for him, and for the first time in months he could think about his father without a suffocating rush of guilt or rage or misery.

'Vicenzu, my darling boy. And Imma too—this is so wonderful!'

The room was suddenly filled with noise, laughter and tears.

'Come on, Mamma, don't cry. I'm here now. These are for you, Zia Carmela.' Kissing his aunt, he handed her some flowers, and then, crouching down, he kissed his mother on both cheeks. 'And these are for you, Mamma,' he said gently, his heart swelling with love and relief as she took the huge bunch of palest pink roses.

Her ankle was a little swollen, and she looked pale, but she was still his mother—and she was smiling now as Imma stepped forward, also smiling shyly.

'And here is my beautiful *nuora*. Imma, thank you so much for coming to see us. I really am so glad you came.'

'Thank you, Signora Trapani—'

'*Mia cara*, call me Audenzia, please. Now, come and sit next to me. Both of you. And you, Carmela. I want to hear all about your beautiful wedding, and of course see the photos. Carlo, will you take these flowers, *per favore*, and put them in water?'

Lazing back in his seat, Vicè watched his mother scroll down through the pictures on his phone, clutching Imma's hand and occasionally wiping away a tear. He felt relaxed, calm and happy. Life had never felt sweeter.

'I would like a copy of this one, Vicenzu.'

His mother was holding up his phone and, glancing at the photo, he felt his pulse stumble. It was a beautiful picture—a close-up, not a selfie. The registrar must have taken it. They were gazing into each other's eyes and there was a sweetness in Imma's face that made him want to pull her into his arms right now and hold her close.

And apologise. Again.

How could he have married her in that two-bit way? He'd let her wear that same dress she'd worn to her sister's wedding and exchanged vows with her in a ceremony that had lasted only slightly longer than it would have taken to open a bottle of Prosecco.

That photo was a beautiful lie, and he was ashamed of being a part of it, but he was even more ashamed of having made her part of it too.

'And this one, too. You look just like when you were a little boy. I have a photo in one of my albums…'

'Maybe after lunch, Mamma,' he said, smiling mechanically at Carlo's expression of despair.

As Carmela led Imma away, to show her the rest of the apartment, his mother took his arm and gave it a quick squeeze.

'I know you must have wanted to give her a more special day, *babà*. But you were in a rush—I understand.'

But she didn't. Not really. He'd seen his parents' wedding album and, although their day had clearly not been as over the top as Ciro and Claudia's, it had been undeniably romantic.

He felt sick with remorse. For a fraction of a second he was glad for the first time that his father was not alive to bear witness to his incompetence and insensitivity.

'I'm sorry, Mamma—' he began, but his mother shook her head.

'For what? Falling in love and wanting your life with Imma to start as soon as possible?' Her eyes were gentle and loving. 'You will make every day from now on special. And you are so *simpatico* together. I wish your father was here to see the two of you. He would be so very happy, and so proud of the man you have become. A man who can love and be loved in return—isn't that how the song goes?' She patted his cheek. 'He loved that song.'

He smiled down at her, but inside he could feel something tearing. It was crazy, but he kept forgetting that he and Imma were not a real couple. Watching her with his mother and aunt, he'd almost forgotten that theirs was a marriage of convenience not love.

Only now his mother was praising him for something he hadn't done, something he wasn't capable of doing, and he felt guilt and panic unfurl inside him.

He knew what his father had wanted him to be. But he wasn't that man and nor could he ever be him. And besides, in the long term Imma wanted her freedom. They both did.

'Oh, Carlo, you clever man! How perfect!' Audenzia looked up at her brother-in-law, her eyes sparkling like the glass of Prosecco he had handed her. 'A toast to my darling son and his beautiful bride. To Vicenzu and Imma. *Cent' anni!*'

A hundred years.

It was just a toast, Imma told herself, glancing at the hibiscus flower at the bottom of her glass of Prosecco. But every time she remembered Audenzia's joyful words she felt a sharp nip of guilt. And something else—something she couldn't quite place.

They had just finished lunch on the balcony overlooking the garden. The food had been sublime and the view was incredible, but she kept losing concentration, her mind returning like a homing pigeon to that moment when Vicè had held up his glass and toasted their marriage.

As his eyes had met hers she'd forgotten to breathe, much less raise her glass. But it wasn't those few shared half seconds that were making her heart pound—it was the memory of that half hour in the car, when he had let his mask slip and needed her for something more than sex.

Audenzia reached out and took her hand. 'Now, Imma, I love my boy, but he has a few tiny faults. He can't have too much red wine. It makes him grumpy.'

Vicè rolled his eyes. 'I'm still here, you know!'

'And he puts too much of that product in his hair.'

Imma giggled.

'And I'm *still* here.' Shaking his head, Vicè grimaced.

'Well, you shouldn't be. Go with Carmela and get my albums. We must show Imma *all* the photos before you leave.'

'Must we?' Groaning, he stood up. 'This is just a ruse to get me out of the room, isn't it?'

'Of course.' His mother smiled. 'We want to talk about you in private. Now, go.' She turned to Imma, her eyes sparkling. 'It's important to keep a man on his toes.' She sighed. 'If only I could show you the garden.'

Imma followed her gaze. 'It's beautiful.'

'Oh, it's not my efforts. Carlo is the gardener—the

same as my Alessandro. He could grow anything. That's why he bought the estate on Sicily.'

Imma managed to keep smiling but her chest felt tight, and maybe something of what she was feeling showed in her face, because Audenzia reached over and patted her hand.

'Oh, child, don't be upset. I loved my life there, but Florence is where I grew up, and I'm happy to be back here. It was different for Alessandro. It was in his blood…in his heart. Vicenzu feels the same way.'

Imma stared at her in confusion. *Did he?* He had never so much as hinted that was how he felt about the estate. On the contrary, he seemed to love his life at La Dolce Vita.

'Did he ever want to take it over?'

'When he was a little boy it was all he talked about. And of course Alessandro wanted that too. But he didn't want to put pressure on him.' Her smile faded. 'Vicenzu idolised his father, only I don't think he ever believed he could step into his shoes so he stopped trying. But Alessandro would be delighted to know the business is still in the family. And to know that Vicenzu has met and married you.' She squeezed Imma's hand. 'You've seen who he really is and you love him.'

Imma nodded. 'Yes, I do.'

She had agreed automatically but her heart swelled as she spoke, opening like the petals of the hibiscus flower in her glass, and with a shock she realised that she wasn't lying or pretending.

She loved Vicè.

Stunned, disbelieving, she repeated the words in her head.

It was true.

Her heart beat a little faster.

And maybe…possibly…he might feel the same way about her.

Okay, he had never said he loved her, but perhaps, like her, it hadn't occurred to him. Perhaps all he needed was someone to point it out to him.

The drive back to Portofino was quicker and quieter than the trip down.

Fixing his eyes on the road, Vicè was aware that he wasn't saying much. But Imma hadn't noticed. In fact, she seemed distracted, wrapped up in her own thoughts, and that was fine.

There had been enough drama for one day.

The villa felt quiet, almost subdued after the laughter and chatter of Florence, and it fed into his mood so that he felt oddly flattened as he walked up to the bedroom. Maybe a swim would help. Or a drink.

'Do you want some wine?' He turned towards Imma, smiling. 'You look like I feel, *cara*. What we need is a couple of late nights.'

She smiled, but it didn't reach her eyes, and the heaviness in his chest seemed to swell and press against his ribs.

'I'm teasing. I know you're tired. I am too. It was a long day.'

She shook her head. 'It's not that. I want to go back to Sicily with you.'

He felt a rush of relief. *Of course*. That was why she was on edge. Seeing his mother had made her homesick. But it was easily fixed. He wasn't willing to see Cesare, but he could visit friends while she saw her father.

'That's fine. We can fly back tomorrow. We can stay for a couple of days—'

She hesitated. 'I don't mean for a visit. I want to move back. To live there. With you.'

'That would be a hell of a commute,' he said lightly.

Glancing down, he saw the tension, the hope in her eyes, and felt his stomach clench.

'What's brought this on?'

'I suppose it was seeing your *mamma*. It made me think about things…about what we're doing…'

He felt suddenly short of breath. 'I know it's hard, having to pretend. I hated lying to her too.'

'But that's just it. I wasn't lying,' she said slowly.

His heart was beating out of time. 'I don't understand—'

Except he did. He knew what she was saying even if she hadn't said the words—he could read it in her eyes.

Looking down into her face, he felt a sudden rush of panic. Her eyes were wide with hope, with trust.

With love.

'You said you'd give me a year so I could find out what I wanted. But I don't need a year, Vicè. I already know what I want. I want us to go back to Sicily together.'

He held her gaze. 'I have a business here—a life. I can't just go back to Sicily.'

'I thought we could run your father's business together.'

Once upon a time that had been his dream. For a fraction of a second he saw the warm olive groves in his head…could almost feel the dry ground beneath his feet. And then he pictured his father's face, the reassuring smile that hid the disappointment in his heart.

He couldn't face seeing that same disappointment on Imma's face.

'I don't want to do that, *cara*. That's why I live here.'

She looked confused—no, more than confused… crushed.

'But… I just… I thought you— We— Your mother—'

He shook his head. 'My mother misses the past. She misses my father. But I'm not my father.'

He felt suddenly furious with Imma. Why was she doing this? Saying these things. Everything had been just fine. Why did she have mess it up?

'I love my life as it is,' he said stiffly.

She jerked back, as though he had hit her, and he knew that her pain was as real as if he *had* hit her. He knew because the pain in his chest hurt so badly it was making him feel ill.

'This year is about helping you. I wanted to do you a favour, that's all,' he lied.

For a moment she seemed too stunned to speak, and then slowly she frowned. 'I don't think I need your help, actually. I can manage just fine on my own.'

The hurt in her voice made his body tense. 'I'm sorry, Imma.'

'Don't be.'

She lifted her chin and he saw the sheen of tears in her eyes. 'We said no more lies, remember? I don't think there's any point in my staying now, do you?'

In the silence that followed her question, her hurt was palpable. But what could he say? *Yes, I want you to stay so we can keep on having sex?*

With an effort, he shook his head, and after a moment, she said quietly, 'If you really don't want the business then I'll sign it back over to my father.' When he didn't respond, she gave him a small, sad smile. 'I'll go and pack.'

He watched her walk upstairs. He'd never known a feeling like this—not even when his mother had called to tell him his father had died. His heart was like a living, struggling creature trapped inside his chest.

Only what choice did he have? He couldn't do to her what he had done to his father. He couldn't be responsible for her love. Nor was he worthy of it. Not when he was so flawed, so imperfect, so bound to mess up.

CHAPTER TEN

'GREAT PARTY, VICÈ!'

Vicè turned, flicking on his hundred-kilowatt smile automatically as the pop-star-turned-actress who was standing in front of him tilted her head in provocation.

'Thanks, Renée—and congratulations on the nomination.' He raised the glass of champagne he was holding. 'There's a bottle of Cristal at the bar with your name on it.'

'Care to come and share it with me?' she invited, her mane of auburn hair falling into her eyes and the hem of her shimmering red minidress riding high on her thighs as she pouted up at him. 'We could have our own private party.'

His pulse accelerated. She was beautiful, willing, and she had booked a suite, and yet…

He shook his head slowly, pretending regret. 'I need to make sure this party keeps rolling, Renée.'

He had never been too hung up dotting the *i*'s and crossing the *t*'s, but mixing business and pleasure was one rule that should never be broken, no matter how much pleasure was being promised.

His chest tightened.

What a load of sanctimonious drivel!

He liked Renée—she was sweet—but he wasn't going to sleep with her, whatever the circumstances. There was only one woman he wanted, and he had let her slip through his fingers just over five weeks ago.

His mouth twisted. Actually, he'd driven her to the airport.

Way to go, Vicè. Drive the woman you love to the airport and wave her off.

His heart was suddenly thumping so hard against his ribs he was surprised the shock waves didn't shatter the glass he was holding.

He *loved* her?

For a moment he turned over his words in his mind, waiting for the denial that would surely follow. Instead, though, the echo grew louder, rebounding and filling his head.

He loved her.

But of course he did.

Only he had pushed her away rather than admit it to himself. Or to her. And now she was gone. And he was going to have to live without her in an agonising charade of his own making for the rest of his life.

'Sorry, Renée. I didn't mean to sound so pompous.' Holding up his hand, he tapped the ring on his finger. 'It's just that I'm missing my wife.'

A flush of colour spread over her face. 'I'm sorry... I didn't know you were—'

'It's fine.' He pasted a smile on his face. 'Look, you have a great night.'

'You too, Vicè.'

She blew him a kiss from her bee-stung mouth and he watched her sashay off on her towering heels.

Eyes burning, he turned away from the laughing,

dancing mass of people. Last time he had been on the yacht Imma had been by his side. Now, without her, he felt empty. Without her all of this—his life, his much-prized *dolce far niente*—was literally nothing.

It was ironic, really. She had told him that she wanted to find herself, and he had blithely told her that he would give her a year, never once realising that *he* was the one who didn't know who he was or what he wanted.

But he did now.

And pushing her away hadn't changed a thing. Wherever she was in the world, she had his heart. He belonged to her. He would always belong to her.

Only it was too late.

Even though all the dots had been there in front of him he had been too scared to connect them—too scared of the picture they would make. So he had let her leave. Worse, he had let her end it. He hadn't even had the courage to do that.

He was a coward and a fool. For in trying to play it cool he had simply succeeded in making his own world a lot colder.

The ache in his heart made him feel sick, but he didn't care. He couldn't lie to himself any more and pretend he felt nothing for Imma. His 'sweet life' tasted bitter now. The pain of loving had been replaced with the pain of loss, as bad as when his father had died.

Closing his eyes, he pictured Alessandro's face. He still missed him—probably he always would. And yet it didn't hurt quite as much as before. The tension in his shoulders eased a little.

Now it wasn't the funeral he remembered, but happier times. Meals round the table. Stories before bedtime. And watching his father dance with his mother,

her head resting against his chest and Alessandro singing softly.

Now he could think about his father without flinching, and that was thanks to Imma. She had helped him grieve and had put words to his unspoken fears so that they had stopped being the terrifying larger-than-life problems he had always refused to face.

Like the words of another of his father's favourite songs, he had let her get under his skin and found he was a better person with her. Or at least good enough for her to confide her own fears.

His heart began to beat a little faster.

Imma had drawn strength from him too. Holding his hand, she had leapt into the unknown. That night on Pantelleria she had even trusted him to take her virginity, and then later entered into a marriage of convenience with him.

She had even trusted him enough to love him.

Staring out across the dark sea, he felt his fingers tighten against his glass.

Maybe it was time he started trusting himself.

Pushing her sunglasses onto the top of her head, Imma stopped beside the market stall. For a moment her hand hovered over a crate overflowing with lemons, and then, changing her mind, she selected a couple of peaches.

Once—a lifetime ago—this would have been her dream. The freedom to wander alone among the colourful stalls, to linger and to chat to people without the continual unsmiling presence of her security team.

But that dream felt childish now, in comparison to the loss of her dream of love with Vicè.

Smiling politely at the tiny, leathery old woman who

ran the stall, she took her change and made her way back past the boutiques and ice-cream parlours.

She had chosen the small town of Cefalù in northern Sicily on a whim, but after nearly five weeks of living here she liked it a lot. It would be a good place to stay while she worked out what to do next.

The villa she was renting was outside the town, a good ten-minute walk away from the noisy hubbub of the market. It was quiet—isolated, even—but right now that was exactly what she wanted. Somewhere quiet, away from the world, where she could lick her wounds.

Thinking back to those horrific last hours with Vicè, she felt a rush of queasiness. She'd been so excited, so caught up in the thrilling realisation of her own love for him, that she'd completely misjudged his feelings. And in the face of his less than enthusiastic response to her suggestion that they take over his father's business together she'd had no option but to face the facts.

He didn't need or want her.

He certainly didn't want her love.

And, to be fair, he hadn't ever offered her a real relationship. As he'd said, he'd only been doing her a favour.

She had wanted to call a taxi, but he had insisted on driving her to the airport. She would never forget that silent, never-ending journey to Genoa.

As they'd left Portofino he had asked her if she wanted to listen to the radio. Then he had asked if she wanted him to turn up the air-conditioning.

At no point had he asked her to stay.

At the airport he had offered to go in with her, but her nerves had been in shreds by then and she had simply shaken her head.

Her throat tightened. He hadn't used his legendary

powers of persuasion to convince her otherwise. Maybe he had been daunted by her silence.

The other, more devastating but more likely explanation was that he had been desperate for her to be gone so that he could get back to the sweet, easy life he'd had before meeting her...

Walking into the villa, she forced herself to unpack her shopping and put it away before checking her phone for messages. At first she had checked it obsessively, but as the hours had turned into days and the days had become weeks she had forced herself not to look.

Before leaving, she had agreed with him that they would say nothing to their families. She couldn't remember who had suggested it, but she was glad. There was no way she could face her father's I-told-you-so reaction—or, worse, his clumsy attempts to try and make amends. Nor did she want to confide in Claudia. She was doing so well right now, and she feared offloading her problems on to her sister would ruin the fragile peace Claudia had found.

Peace, and happiness at the discovery she was having a baby.

Her breath twisted in her throat.

She had wanted to go to her, of course, but Claudia had been firm and, hearing the flicker of determination in her voice, Imma had understood that her sister needed to prove she could cope alone.

So she had carried on speaking to both of them every couple of days, acting as if nothing had happened, making sure that the conversation merely touched on Vicè.

Her stomach clenched. Against her will she was living another charade, and it was only through sheer effort of will that she dragged herself out of bed each morning, got dressed and made herself eat breakfast.

Incredibly, the one person she found herself wanting to talk to was Audenzia. During those few hours in Florence she had found herself admiring her quiet strength and love of life.

Under other circumstances she would have liked to get to know her better.

But now, of course, that was impossible.

Almost as impossible as stopping all these incessant what-if and if-only thoughts.

Glancing out of the window, she felt her heartbeat slow. She couldn't see Portofino from the villa, but that didn't stop her from closing her eyes and imagining. *What would he be doing right now?*

Opening her eyes, she pushed the thought away before it could spiral out of control. Each morning she promised herself that she wouldn't think about Vicè until lunchtime, and today she had almost managed it—that was something to celebrate.

In fact, she *was* going to celebrate. She was going to take her lunch to the beach and have a picnic. Even though the 'beach' was not really a beach at all—more a patch of sand in a rocky alcove.

After she'd finished eating, she watched the Palermo to Naples ferry heading off towards the mainland. It made her feel calmer, thinking about all those people on board, with all their hopes and dreams buzzing inside their heads.

Her heart might have been broken by Vicè but that didn't mean her life was over. She was going to be all right. He might not love her, but she couldn't regret the time they had spent together. He had taught her to be brave, to take risks.

Yes, she loved him still. Maybe she always would. But she was ready to face the world. On her terms.

Standing up, she brushed the sand off her legs and began to walk carefully across the rocks and back up to the house. But as she reached the villa her feet suddenly faltered.

A man was waiting for her.

Her heart began to pound.

Not because he was a stranger.

But because he wasn't.

She stared at him, stunned and furious. Even if she wanted to run—and she did—nothing seemed to be functioning. Instead she stood woodenly while Vicè walked slowly towards her.

How had he found her? And, more importantly, why was he here?

He had no right to come here—not when she was finally beginning to get him out of her head, if not her heart, she thought as he stopped in front of her, his dark hair blowing in the breeze.

He was dressed incongruously, in a dark suit and shirt, only it wasn't his clothing that made her throat tighten. But she had learned from her mistakes, and she wasn't ever going to let herself be distracted by his beauty again.

'Hi,' he said softly.

She lifted her chin. 'How did you find me?'

'With great difficulty.' He smiled, and then, when she didn't smile back, he shrugged. 'My lawyer Vito knows some people who keep their ears to the ground. He uses them to find clients that skip bail.'

'And I thought it was my father who had the shady friends.'

His expression didn't change—but then why should it? If he had ever cared what she thought of him, he certainly didn't any more.

'Why are you here, Vicè? I mean, I take it this isn't a social call?'

'I had a meeting with Vito this morning.' He stared at her steadily. 'I had some paperwork to complete.'

Inside her head his words were bumping into one another in slow motion, like a train and its carriages hitting the buffers. Glancing down, she saw that he was holding an envelope. Her heart shrivelled in her chest. *Paperwork*. In other words, he wanted a divorce.

Pain seared every nerve. 'I thought you were giving me a year?'

He glanced away. 'I can't wait that long.'

She wanted to scream and shout and rage—at the unfairness of life and at the unknowable cruelty of loving someone who didn't love you. But she had laid enough of her feelings bare to this man.

'Fine. Just give me the paperwork and I'll sign it.'

'It's already signed.'

He took a step closer and she backed away from him, not caring that he could see her pain, just wanting him gone.

'Your father signed it this morning.'

She stared at him in confusion—and then suddenly she understood. 'You came back for the business. That's why you came to Sicily. For your father's business.'

He stared at her, his gaze steady and unflinching. 'He signed it over to me this morning.'

Why did it hurt so much? She'd known right from

the start that he'd only ever wanted that. Whatever he'd said in the car on the way to Florence and then at the villa, it obviously was still.

Her chest tightened.

But why had her father agreed to hand it over? Had Vicenzu told him the truth about their marriage? Even though he knew what it would mean for her.

'Did you tell him about us?' she asked slowly.

He shook his head.

'Then how—'

His eyes met hers. 'I threatened him. I told him I had enough on him to make sure he'd lose everything he cared about. Just like my father did.'

On one level she knew her father deserved it, but it hurt hearing Vicè talk in that way.

'Blackmail and extortion? That sounds more like my father than you.'

'I said all that afterwards.' He ran an agitated hand through his hair. 'First I met him for breakfast. I told him that I wanted to buy back the business and that I would pay what he thought was a fair price.'

'What...?' Imma felt as if she was in a daze.

'I'm not like your father, *cara*. I don't bully or blackmail people into doing what I want. I paid him what he asked—twice what he paid my father—so that you and I can start with a clean sheet.'

Her heart was in her mouth. 'I don't understand...'

'You asked me why I was here.' His eyes found hers. '*You're* why. I've bought the business back. For us.'

She shook her head. 'There is no us.'

'There is. Only it took you leaving for me to see it.' He took another step closer. 'I love you, Imma. And

I want to be with you. Not for the cameras, or for the business, but because you're in my heart.'

His voice was shaking now, and she could see tears in his eyes.

'You helped me find out what and who I want to be. And I want to be your husband. For real. Forever.'

Reaching out, he took her hands.

'I'm sorry I didn't stop you leaving, but when you said you wanted us to run the business together I panicked. I mess up all the time, *cara*—with family, with work, with you. And I've hurt people, you especially, and I didn't want to hurt you any more. I don't ever want to hurt you.'

He shook his head.

'I should never have let you go. But I thought that making you stay would have just been me being selfish—that it was what the old Vicè would have done. And I wanted to be a better man. So I let you go and I pretended everything was cool.'

His mouth twisted.

'Only it wasn't. I missed you like crazy. So I went and saw Mamma and I told her everything.'

'Everything?' Her eyes widened with shock.

'Everything. I was sick and tired of lying to everyone. To her...to you. To myself.'

Screwing up his face, he shook his head.

'I think it's the first time she's ever lost her temper with me. *Cavolo*, she was mad at me. Like, furious. Every time I thought she'd finished she'd start up again. She told me she was ashamed of me, that my father would be ashamed of me, and then she told me I had to put it right.'

Imma bit her lip and, reaching out, placed her hands

against his chest, feeling his heart beating into her fingertips. 'Did you tell her about what my father did?'

He pulled her closer. 'A bit.'

'Is that why you threatened him? For your *mamma*?'

'No. I wanted him to know what it felt like to be cornered and helpless.' He gave her a small crooked smile. 'And then I made him donate a lot of money to my mother's favourite charity. Weirdly, it was the difference between what he paid my father and what I paid him.'

She smiled. 'That won't have helped his heart.'

'*What* heart?'

He gazed down into her eyes and she felt her own heart flutter inside her chest.

'I thought I wasn't worthy of your love, *cara*. Probably I'm not. But I'm going to do whatever it takes to be worthy.'

'So you don't want a divorce?' she asked softly.

'*No.*' He stared down at her, his arms tensing around her. 'Do you?'

She shook her head and, breathing out unsteadily, he buried his face in her hair.

'In that case, I have something for you.' Reaching into his jacket, he pulled out a small square box. 'You never had an engagement ring, so I thought I'd get you an eternity ring instead.' His eyes were bright. 'That's how long I want to be with you. For eternity.'

Tears slid down her cheeks as he opened the box and slipped a beautiful emerald ring onto her finger. 'Oh, Vicè...'

Laughing softly, he wiped her tears away with his thumbs. 'I had some change left over...it was that or blow it all in a high-stakes poker game—'

'Change from what?' She looked up at him in confusion.

He hesitated, and she felt the muscles in his arms tighten.

'I sold the Dolce.'

She gaped at him. 'You *sold* it? But why?'

'I needed the money to buy the business back. It was that or go to Ciro.' He grimaced. 'So, as I say, I needed the money.'

'But you love the Dolce.'

'I did—I do. And I've kept a stake in it. But I don't need it any more.'

His gaze rested on her face, and his love was there for anyone to see.

'You're the sweetness in my life, *cara*.' His eyes dropped to the ring sparkling on her finger. 'Now and for eternity.'

EPILOGUE

IT WAS A hot day in late September—one of the hottest on record, according to Manfredi, the Trapani estate's longest-serving member of staff. But the weather was the last thing on Imma's mind as she walked slowly through the olive trees.

She had spoken to Claudia that morning, and her sister's news had pushed every other thought out of her head.

Almost every other thought.

But right now that would have to wait.

Breathing in the scent of warm earth and grass, she replayed her conversation with Claudia.

Claudia and Ciro were together. They were in love. Both of them this time.

It was a lot to take in—too much for one person on her own.

A tremble of happiness ran over her skin.

But she wasn't on her own any more.

Her eyes fixed on the group of men standing beneath the trees at the other side of the olive grove. Or rather on one particular man.

Vicè was gesticulating energetically, his dark eyes moving over the other men's faces as he spoke, and she felt a sharp, almost unbearable urge to push them all aside and drag him back to the villa and upstairs to their bedroom.

'Imma!'

She looked up at the sound of his voice, her heart leaping as it still did, maybe three, five, sometimes ten times a day, whenever she remembered that Vicè was her husband 'for real' and 'forever'.

Pulse jumping, she watched him excuse himself, and then he was walking towards her, his long legs making short work of the uneven ground and a slow, curling smile pulling at the corners of his mouth.

She felt her stomach flutter. She had thought that he couldn't look any more desirable than he did in a suit, but she'd been wrong. In scuffed work boots, faded chinos, and with the sleeves of his denim shirt rolled up he looked impossibly sexy.

'Signora Trapani...'

He pulled her against him, his mouth seeking hers with an urgency that made her whole body twitch with desire.

Behind them, a cacophony of approving whistles and shouts filled the air.

'Vicè, everyone is watching us,' she whispered.

'So let them watch. I'm just saying good morning to my wife.'

His voice was warm, and she felt an answering warmth across her skin.

Her eyes met his. 'You did that already.'

The corner of his mouth tugged upward. 'I'm thinking that was more of a *ciao* than a *buongiorno*.' His dark gaze drifted slowly over her face. 'How do you feel about going back to the villa and brushing up on our greetings?'

'It wouldn't hurt,' she said softly. 'I mean, just because we're married it doesn't mean we should take each other for granted…'

Watching the flush of colour suffuse her cheeks, Vicè felt his body harden. That she should want him at all still felt like a miracle, but that she loved him…

There were no words that could adequately capture how that made him feel. All he knew was that he was the luckiest man in the world.

The doubts and regrets of the past were forgotten now. Imma loved him, and he knew that her love and the efforts he'd made to deserve it would have earned his father's respect.

Life had never been sweeter.

Uncurling his arm from around her waist, he took her hand and led her back across the field.

'I like this dress.' His eyes ran over the curve of her breast. 'Although I think it will look even better once you've taken it off.'

She smiled, hesitated, then said, 'Claudia called.'

Cavolo. He swore silently.

'Yeah, Ciro called me too.' He'd been so caught up in this morning's meeting he'd actually momentarily forgotten about his brother's call. 'He sounded pretty happy. Is that how Claudia sounded?'

She nodded. 'It's all she's ever wanted, but—'

'But what?' Turning towards her, he caught her chin. 'What is it, *cara*?'

Her green eyes were so open, so unguarded, and he felt a sudden urge to tell her how much he loved her, how necessary she was for his own happiness. But he didn't need to say anything. She already knew, and that made him love her even more.

'You can tell me.'

She bit her lip. 'It *is* real, isn't it? This time? He does love her? I mean, he's not just saying it because your *mamma*—'

He hated seeing her so worried—hated that he had something to do with her doubts.

Pulling her closer, he shook his head. 'Mamma didn't speak to him until after he and Claudia had sorted it out between them. You don't need to worry, *cara*. Honestly, I've never heard my brother sound like that before. He's crazy about her.'

Ciro had been so emotional. For once, he had actually felt like the big brother.

His fingers tightened around hers. 'I promise it's real, *cara*. As real as you and I. All of what happened—it's in the past for Ciro, for me.'

It was a past that didn't feel so much like another country to him as a different planet.

'I feel the same way,' she said.

He stroked her cheek. 'Have they told anyone else?'

'Claudia told Papà.' Her eyes met his. 'But she agreed that the same rules I insisted on will apply.'

Vicè nodded. Imma had gone to see Cesare the day after they had got back together. Glancing down at her beautiful face, he felt a rush of pride in his wife for facing up to the man who had once dominated her whole life.

She'd given her father an ultimatum: change, or she and Claudia would cut him out of their lives forever.

And Cesare had capitulated. In fact, he had blubbed

like a child, apologised, and then made promises which, so far, he was keeping.

'Why are you smiling like that?' she asked slowly.

'I was just thinking what a great aunt you'll be, Zia Imma. Of course I'll be the most fantastic uncle too.'

She laughed. 'That won't be hard as you'll be the only uncle.' Her face softened. 'Vicè, if you're half as good at being an uncle as you are at being a husband and a boss, you'll be better than fantastic.'

'Let's see if you still think that after the harvest,' he said lightly.

'I will.' Her eyes met his. 'I spoke to Manfredi this morning. He said that you have the same feel for the olives as your father.'

He felt his heart contract.

Stepping into his father's shoes had been nerve-racking. He still had doubts about his ability to pull it off. But with Imma by his side . .

He felt a fierce, unpremeditated quiver of anticipation. She was his partner, his equal. Together they had already faced their fears. And together they would meet whatever happened in the future.

Watching the mix of sadness and pride in Vicè's eyes, Imma felt her heart swell.

She knew how much this estate meant to him. It was his father's legacy and one day it would be his.

Her breath caught in her throat.

'So, are you going to be Zio Vicenzu or Zio Vicè?'

'Not Vicenzu.' He shuddered. 'Too serious. Vicè is what a cool uncle would be called, and I am definitely going to be a cool uncle.' His eyes gleamed. 'I cannot wait until this baby is born. Hopefully he's going to be just like me. That'll keep Ciro on his toes.'

'It might not be a boy.'

'It is.'

She raised an eyebrow. 'And you know this how, exactly?'

'Man's intuition.' He grinned. 'It's very rare—only the most impressive males of the species have it.'

'Right... And I'm guessing it's infallible?'

He nodded, and keeping her expression innocent, she took his hand and rested it gently on her stomach. 'So what are *we* having, then?'

He stilled, his eyes widening with shock. 'You're pregnant?'

She nodded. 'I did a test after Claudia rang. Actually, I did two. Just to be sure.'

'And it's definite?'

She drew a deep breath and nodded again. 'I was going to wait for the perfect moment to tell you, but then I realised that every moment is perfect with you.'

There was a shake in her voice that matched the tremble in his hands as they tightened around hers.

Looking up, she bit her lip. 'Are you pleased?'

'Pleased?' His eyes filled with tears. 'I'm ecstatic.'

He pulled her against him, burying his face in her hair, pressing her close to his heart, which was hammering as wildly as hers.

'You're having my baby.'

He kissed her gently on the lips and she felt his mouth curve into a grin.

'Of course, with my man's intuition I already knew that—'

She punched him lightly on the arm. 'You are such a bad liar, Vicenzu Trapani.'

'Thanks to you,' he said softly.

His smile sent a shiver of heat down her spine. 'I love you, Vicè.'

Tipping her mouth up to his, he kissed her again. 'I love you too, Imma. That's the truth and it's going to stay true forever.'

She felt her pulse twitch as he gazed down at her, his dark eyes gleaming.

'That dress, though—that's coming off right now.'

And, scooping her up into arms, he carried her into the villa and upstairs to their bedroom.

* * * * *

Swept away by Louise Fuller's
The Terms of the Sicilian's Marriage?
Discover the first instalment in
The Sicilian Marriage Pact *duet*
A Baby to Bind His Innocent *by Michelle Smart*
Available now!

And why not lose yourself in these other
Louise Fuller stories?

Demanding His Secret Son
Consequences of a Hot Havana Night
Proof of Their One-Night Passion
Craving His Forbidden Innocent

All available now!